H4

I thought she'd move away. But her hands hovered above my shoulders — like birds whose flight has been stopped by a sudden wind.

Then her hands were in my hair, her lips on my throat, on my eyes, my mouth. With a flash of desire like lightning, I was swept into the hot storm of her love.

Its thunder roared in my ears as she drew her tongue along my lips and moved her fingers lightly down my back. I pulled the pearl-tipped pins out of her stola and stepped back as she shrugged it off to stand naked before me. Her body was the color of fresh cream. Almost without volition, I dropped to my knees and buried my face in her belly to taste its sweet warmth. My womb leapt as she put her hands in my hair, then slid them down to cup my breasts. I moved toward the dark hair of her mons . . .

AVALON

AVALON

BY MARY J. JONES

The Naiad Press, Inc.
1991

Printed in the United States of America on acid-free paper
First Edition

Edited by Katherine V. Forrest
Cover design by Pat Tong and Bonnie Liss
    (Phoenix Graphics)
Typeset by Sandi Stancil

Library of Congress Cataloging-in-Publication Data

Jones, Mary J., 1938–
    Avalon / by Mary J. Jones
        p.   cm.
    ISBN 0-941483-96-7 : $9.95
    I. Arthurian romances--Adaptations.   I. Title.
PS3560.05224A93   1991
813'.54--dc20   91-23639
                                                        CIP

For E. "Five!"

About the Author

Mary J. Jones lives on the seacoast of Iowa.

Prologue

The Queen of the Wastelands sat waiting. Over and over she plucked at a strand of pale gold hair. And, though the hearth-fire burned strongly, she shivered a little, too, there in the rock and ice of her northern fortress. The Queen — she was called Annis — tossed a handful of spices into the fire. Soon the waiting would be done. Soon she would have the means to make the Celtic Realms hers. Hers alone.

Annis gazed at the rings that gleamed darkly on her fingers. In the stone of the darkest of them, she saw a beach far to the south. Onto that beach, out of *a blood-red sunrise, would soon come the two riders who carried what she sought. Already she could hear their horses' hooves pounding along the Roman road. And behind them, the sounds of her own Grey Host, shaped as horsemen now.*

She swept her white cloak up across her shoulders. On the beach, a mist arose.

The two riders reached the rocks at the edge of the sea still ahead of Annis's Host. But the Grey Ones were close. Their battle shouts rang out above the roar of the surf and the rasp of the horses' breath. The two urged their tired mounts onto the beach. There, through the mist, they saw a pair of carraghs pulled just out of the water. In front of the boats stood Fand, Chief Child Gatherer of Avalon, waiting with a dozen or so of the Daughters.

"Greetings, Lancelot, from the Lady and the Nine," Fand said to the taller of the two, touching the knuckle of her index finger to her lips. "And to you, Meredydd," she added with a brief glance at his ginger-haired companion.

They dismounted quickly and, from under his tartan cloak, Lancelot pulled a swaddled but angry baby. "Take her and go!" He thrust the child into Fand's arms.

Deliberately, Fand pulled the linen cover from the howling baby's face and gave a sharp, satisfied nod. "She's alive anyway. Though only the Mother knows how after the ride the two of you probably gave her."

Meredydd shifted her shoulders uneasily. Why

was Fand dawdling? Didn't she understand what hunted this child — and them all? And how could this old woman, even at a moment like this, make her, a king's heir and a warrior who had herself carried the Red Dragon Shield in a score of battles — how could Fand still make her feel like a very nasty little girl? Meredydd noticed that beneath his dark mustache, Lancelot's mouth twitched. She reckoned Fand made him uneasy, too.

They'd ridden most of the night to bring the baby to Fand and, before that, three days from Camelot to Dun Cador to save her from Arthur's rage. For this was Gwenhyfar's child, born four months earlier, and wanted by what was behind them. Not the Pendragon's men now, but the Grey Host, who belonged to someone, something, else.

"Who wrapped this infant? You, Lancelot? Or one of those moronic slave girls Gwenhyfar surrounds herself with? Most likely Gwenhyfar herself, indolent female that she is." The old Gatherer gave them a black glare and began to loosen the swaddling clothes.

The clatter and curses of the Grey Host grew louder. Their stink filled the air. Lancelot, though, could but stare at the wailing baby. Desperate, Meredydd looked through the thickening fog toward the Daughters. A few nervous young girls clustered around the larger of the carraghs. They would row the craft bearing the child across the breakers into open sea. Young as they were, Meredydd was confident they would get the child to the safety of Avalon.

A few yards ahead of them a unit of seasoned warriors was drawn up in fighting order to offer cover. Meredydd had been in battle with Avalon's Daughters more than once — both she and Lancelot had been fostered on the island — and she was glad they would have a pack of those sea-wolves at their backs when they faced the Grey Ones.

Heartened, she returned her attention to Lancelot and Fand. The old woman was still fussing over the baby. Lancelot was sweating hard. "Couldn't you do that in the boat later?" he asked, his voice tight, eyes now on the rocks that marked the end of the Roman road.

"Is this your child, Lancelot?"

Lancelot pulled at the silver torque circling his gritty neck and fingered the Dragon Seal embossed at its ends. "The baby is Gwenhyfar's. It does not matter who her father is."

"What is her name?"

"I believe Gwenhyfar called her Gwyar."

Fand snorted. She looked toward the fog-shrouded sea. "She will be called Argante — brilliant one."

Lancelot started to protest, but Meredydd laid a hand on his arm. This might not be the time for Fand's odd humor, but she did have a right to name the girl. Avalon's Chief Child Gatherer had the right to name any child the Gatherers preserved.

"Must she take so much time about it, though?" Lancelot muttered.

"I've held many infants, including most of those girls —" Fand gestured toward the waiting Daughters. "But there's something about this one. There's a destiny on her, I think."

"Her destiny'll be immediate death. And ours, too,

if you don't get her in that boat." Lancelot grabbed for the baby. Fand snatched her out of reach.

"Not for a long, long time. But something —" The old Gatherer, her head cocked sideways so that she looked like a small, black bird, peered down at the child. "Something —"

Fand turned to the young Daughters at the carragh. "You, Briga. Get over here and take this baby."

A tall, fleshy, red-haired girl trotted across the shingle. Good-looking, Meredydd thought, in a big, awkward way.

"Guard this one with your life," Fand said, handing Briga the baby. "If any harm comes to her, you'll answer to me. Hear?" Gingerly, Briga took the baby into her arms. "Now get out of here. Run, you stupid wench. Go!"

Meredydd would have liked to watch the girl all the way to the boat. But at that moment a dozen mounted warriors emerged from the fog. Meredydd and Lancelot drew their swords; the Daughters closed ranks.

Up in the Wastelands, Annis still gazed into her dark ring, watched as the blood of her Grey Host soaked into the beach and their limbs fell to pieces on the rocks. The carragh bearing Arthur's child was well out to sea. It would be in Avalon before she could summon new troops. She pulled at a strand of hair and thought of raising a storm. But then, looking up, she caught a glimpse of her scowling image in the ice of the walls. Ugly, she thought, and smoothed her hair. Besides, there will come another time, another way.

Annis laughed and her laughter echoed through the corridors of ice like the sound of a distant bell.

Chapter One

Away to the west of Ireland lie what men call the Isles of the Blessed. Here the great heroes of the Celtic Realms come after battle — to rest, to heal, sometimes to die. I am sovereign of one of these islands, that one which is called the Island of the Apples or the Island of Women. We call it Avalon.

I am Argante, Lady of the Lake. It is the third year of my reign, the twenty-fourth of my life. I was brought to Avalon when Lile was Lady; she who died in the Great Hall of Camelot, murdered by one of Arthur's own companions. Before her, Elaine bore the black Lady-mark, and before her, Morgan. There have been Ladies ruling Avalon time out of mind. We are chosen by the Great Mother to serve Her and to watch over the people of the mainlands, the Celtic Realms in Ireland, Britain, and Gaul. It is possible I will be the last Lady of the Lake.

For there is drought in Avalon. As there has been almost since my Lady-making. For each of the last three years, the crops have failed. In the second year, the forests burned. Last autumn, we slaughtered the herds. The winter has been dry.

From my window in the Lady Hall, I look down across the wide triple terrace, with its shrines and gardens, withered now, toward the Crystal City. It has the forlorn look of the abandoned Roman towns on the British mainland. The marketplace is empty, its shops and stalls shut. No laughter rings from the baths, no shouts from the parade ground. Everywhere there is only the sound of the cold, dry wind.

And drought brings disease. Already fifty or sixty people have died coughing up their lungs. Even those still able to work are weak and sick. They go about their duties in the half-stupor of terror. Who can blame them? That there isn't anarchy, as there is on the mainlands where Arthur's wars have loosed the wolf of famine, can only be attributed to the Mother's blessing. Even so, the Potters' wheels have stopped and the Smiths' fires gone out. In the City, Warriors lie dying in their barracks; in the country, Herders perish in their huts. The fishing fleet is two weeks overdue; I don't expect to see them again.

The House of Healing has become a house of death. When I rode out to it yesterday — it sits perhaps a mile beyond the City walls — I found only two Healers still alive. Two women no longer young, and one already marked with the disease's dry cough, trying to cope with more than twenty of the dying and as many dead. I helped bury some of the corpses, which for want of grave-diggers were beginning to rot even at the cemetery gates. It was a hopeless task and I finally ordered the rest taken to sea. I can see the funeral ships now.

I believe, I know, this terrible time is Annis's doing. She would destroy Avalon to destroy our Goddess, her sister. And at last gain dominion over the Celtic Realms for herself alone.

Where is our Goddess, our Mother, in this time of need? Perhaps She has taken another form. The Mother and all the gods take many shapes for They live in many things — in rocks and cows, salt and dragons, steel and children. Nor does Babd, the third sister, hear my prayers. Babd's power lies in her Cauldron, from which the Realms draw all wisdom and inspiration. It may be that Annis has captured the Cauldron, as she tried to capture me.

Or perhaps on a distant, misty mountain Babd and the Goddess wage battle with Annis. I hope, I believe, it is so, for this terrible time can only be Annis's doing. Only Annis could reduce us to this as I have seen her, with a wave of her hand, reduce a field of corn to yellow stubble.

It appears that once again, Avalon does battle with Annis. And we do it alone. We cannot rely on the mainlanders; they cannot bring us food. Nor will they send us prayers. They've been swept away in the red storm of war. And by Christianity.

Arthur has failed them. As he failed the Mother.

Now the mainlands reap his stunted crop. I can do no more for them; Avalon can do no more. Though we still send them swords and horses for their endless wars against the English, or *did* before this drought, these mainlanders have forsaken the Mother. Because of Arthur. In his arrogance and self-absorption — and without his sister Morgant — he has failed them for all time. Not ten years after he took up the steel sword of Avalon, he has led them only to savagery and perpetual warfare. Soon they will be as chaff in the wind: it will be as if they never were.

Annis and her dark powers have won on the mainlands. She used a man-god's religion and an alien race. On Avalon, we have been immune to the religion and the English warriors. Our flesh, though, is subject to what our spirits are not. Annis may win here, too.

So — it is indeed possible I will be the last Lady of the Lake. So — I take time to record the history of my life and reign because it must be done and there is no singer to do it for me. Too many Poets have died already; we buried another two days ago on a lonely spit of land that the sea will overtake before too many years have passed. She was Edain of the Two Harps, a girl hardly past the Mother Choice, but with a splendid voice. Now I fear no sweet-voiced bard will ever stand in the Lady Hall to tell the Daughters — if any survive — how it was with me.

My mother was Gwenhyfar, my father Lancelot or Arthur. I do not know which. Neither did my mother. She leaned toward Lancelot, but only, I think, because she loved him more. I resemble her:

the same plain, square face, the same fair hair and high thin nose, but I have grey eyes, like Arthur. On the other hand, I am tall, much taller than my mother, taller even than Arthur. And Lancelot is very tall. In the end, I suppose it doesn't matter whose child I am. Neither wished to claim me — Lancelot because he wanted to spare my life (so my mother said) and Arthur because he thought me Lancelot's child.

But Arthur and Gwenhyfar and Lancelot — their stories are on the lips of every second-rate singer in three lands. It's *my* tale I must tell. Of my war with Annis, of her curse on me and on Avalon. And I will tell of Elin. Especially of Elin.

I dreamed about Elin last night and about the last time I saw her, our love already forfeit in Arthur's service. And, if I'm honest, in Avalon's as well. Once again, I saw the wild geese overhead, saw myself snatch up the horse's reins and ride away. Once again, I saw her tears and would not stop them.

In the dream I did stop them. I threw down the reins. The geese flew on without me. And Elin ran laughing into my arms. I woke laughing with her.

But when I opened my eyes, it was Deirdre, my aide, who has never laughed waking or sleeping, standing before me. She looked anxious (as I say, laughter worries her). "Are you all right, Lady?" says she in that oily manner she mistakes for courtesy.

"Of course I'm all right, you fool. Go back to bed and leave me to my dreams," I answered, pushing her away. Then I remembered Avalon. "List me the dead."

"The reports from the countryside are not yet in,"

Deirdre said. "Ten in the City." After she had named them and we had spoken of their funeral rites, I ordered her to get me vellum and ink.

"But Lady, you've not strength enough to write." Yesterday, before I left for the House of Healing, she told me I'd not strength to ride.

"Bring me hide, ink. Writing tools. My lap desk. And — don't argue — cider."

Deirdre stared at me, green eyes popping more than usual. She's an ugly thing, especially so just then, with her grey hair creeping out of its stringy braids and her big feet splayed out on my goatskin rug. "Your health —" she began.

"Go! I'm still Lady here, though we all may be dead tomorrow. And don't bother waking up the whole Hall to tell them Argante's gone mad at last. Just do as I say." I'm afraid I grinned at her sullen back as she shuffled out the door.

But when she'd gone I fell back on the pillow, too exhausted to do anything but think of Elin again. Of how I'd left her there in the British mountains and returned to Avalon. And how she'd gone to fight in Arthur's doomed Irish war. And not come back.

I slammed my fist into the bed's pine frame and threw off the fur and linen that covered me. Perhaps my words could call her to me again. As my tears never have.

So — I've polished up my rusty Latin and now sit writing in a wicker chair drawn close to the hearth, an old Roman cavalry blanket spread over my knees. Deirdre calls the blanket a disgrace and I reckon it is pretty ragged. But I slept under it with Elin and I mean to die under it.

12

I've spoken of Arthur and Lancelot, but that I took up the sword and the branch to become Lady of the Lake had nothing to do with my father, whoever he may have been. It has only to do with the Goddess, for ignorance of one's father (or mother, for that matter) is a common condition on Avalon. More than half our population has come here through the Child Gatherings, when, as infants, we are plucked off the moor or mountain where we have been left to die. As a result, we are of all bloods on Avalon: Celtic, Roman, Norse, African, even English. Whatever kind of human jetsam has been tossed onto the shores of the mainlands, its progeny is here. I am a Celt, but Deirdre, in spite of her Irish name, is probably pure English (which may go far to explain her sour nature).

When measured against the mainlands, the Island is a very small place indeed. It is at most a two-day ride from the Far Hills in the north to the Forest of Light in the south. One can ride the width in less than a day. But though our island is only a speck on the ocean, the sea has been kind to us. It is quiet off our shores and full of cod and tuna and mackerel. Its waves do not batter our low sandstone cliffs nor do fierce Atlantic storms smash our trees and villages. Winters, of course, are often harsh, with howling bitter winds and deep wet snow. But they are, as a rule, short and spring comes like a mother, bearing lambs and apple blossoms. We are indeed Goddess-kissed. Or, *were.*

About a thousand people live — lived, I should say — on Avalon, mostly women, but some men, too. Two hundred or so of us are attached to the Lady Hall or live in the Crystal City that clings to its stone feet. Another fifty are very young children fresh from the Gathering who live in a wing of the Hall called the Nursery. There are also older children within the Hall's compound, the young savages, male and female, between the ages of eight and fourteen who make up the Child Corps. It is to the Child Corps that mainland girls and boys are often sent as fosterlings so that they may learn the arts of war with the mysteries of the Mother. Lancelot came here as a child. As did Elin.

The rest of Avalon's people are spread through the Island in villages where each lives with her soul-friend, the companion to whom she swore her life under the blood-red moon of August. They work as Gardeners, who care for the apple orchards and the grain, or Herders, who tend the cattle, sheep, and horses. There are also Timber-women in the forests at the end of the Island and Miners in the hills. In fact, we have all occupations — Poet, Smith, Carpenter. The only things we don't have are bondage and slavery. No matter what we were at birth, prince or peasant, on Avalon we are all free.

And, I might add, free to leave the island at any time. When, for instance, those men who are Gatherlings come of age, they usually choose not to remain on Avalon. They are given cattle enough to establish themselves and sent wherever they wish on the mainlands. There, they are not considered clanless men as other strangers are, but men under the special watch of the Goddess. They are welcomed and honored wherever they go. Many of them served in the Roman legions and with Ambrosius and Uther. Arthur's army is swelled with them.

No one was more surprised than I when the

Mother chose me to rule over this diverse populace, though a good many people were very surprised indeed. Nothing in my girlhood or youth seemed to foretell such a future for me. I began, along with every other child the Gatherers bring us, in the Nursery. There, we were, and still are, loved and taught by the oldest women of Avalon, the *nainau*, whose duties as Smiths and Herders, Warriors or Weavers have come to an end. These are the women from whom we learn to speak and to love. It is they who bind our scraped knees and kiss away our bad dreams.

I remember the *nainau* of my childhood so well that sometimes when I visit the Nursery now, I wonder where Duan is, whose old green Gatherer's robe always had a sweet hidden somewhere in its folds. Where is Cerridwen, that aging but untamed Warrior who played every game and ran every race to win on the excuse that children had to understand defeat before they could understand victory?

When we were about four or five, too young yet for the Child Corps but too old to be constantly underfoot, we were all but given the freedom of the Crystal City. We could meander through the Lady's gardens or paddle in the ornamental fish pools watched only by a bored twelve-year-old being punished for some minor infraction of the Child Corps rules. Of course, by then we had our duties — waving birds out of the fields in the summer and filling kindling boxes in the winter — but it was an easy, sun-filled childhood.

One day when I was about seven was *not* so sun-filled. My section of the Nursery stood together on the porch of the Lady Hall, rain dripping slowly from its thatched eaves.

"Concentrate, girl," Cerridwen bawled at me. "Even you shouldn't have any trouble learning this. It's that simple."

We were learning the art of shape-shifting. Already Faencha and Branwen had managed to become small red birds. I watched them bathe in a puddle, then sit preening themselves in the shelter of the porch.

Shape-shifting is not an unusual skill on Avalon. Almost all the women know how and a good many of the men. It's considered a minor accomplishment, somewhere between being able to snatch an egg from under a setting hen without disturbing her and plucking a sheep smooth. And we learn it young. One of the *nainau* teaches it on a rainy afternoon when there's nothing of more importance to be done.

"Concentrate," Cerridwen bawled again, her lined old face twisted with disgust.

But I couldn't, though concentration was apparently what it took. Every time Cerridwen showed us the technique — "Believe in a red bird. Imagine it flying. Believe yourself flying, believe in the wind and the rain against your wings. Now lift, fly, soar, little ones!" — one or the other of the rest did. I stood and watched them swooping above the City, out over the bay. First Faencha and Branwen. Then Carlin and Orna. Finally, even the boys.

But not me. My concentration was always broken. By a yellow cat prowling among the camellias, the creak of a passing cart, a grease spot on my tunic. Almost anything distracted me. Even when Cerridwen took me alone to a deserted tract of beach, I could think of nothing but the fact that there was a grain of sand in my shoe.

After a week or so, Cerridwen gave up. "You're one of the *cleifion*," she said. The *cleifion* are those Gatherlings who cannot be saved even on Avalon: the ones who come with heads too big or too small, or with slanted eyes and tongues they can't keep in their mouths. They die young or spend their lives being led by their sectionmates.

I fled up to the orchards, where I hid until early evening when my friend Faencha came to find me. She tried to comfort me, but I could sense the suppressed superiority in her and would have none of it. She went away, looking hurt, and a little later Nimue sought me out.

Nimue was fourteen, Chief Centurion of the Child Corps, and a great favorite of mine. Nimue was immensely popular with all the children in the Nursery. She was always sweet-voiced with us, unlike the rest of the Child Corps, who liked to lord it over the little ones. Or maybe her tiny stature made her less frightening than did the soaring heights of the other fourteen-year-olds. And, of course, we thought she was beautiful — blonde as a Saxon, but with eyes of soft chestnut.

"Don't feel so bad, Argante," she said, settling herself next to me where I lay under an apple tree. "Being able to turn yourself into a bird isn't so important. You've got lots of other talents."

"What?"

"Well —" Nimue thought for a long moment. "Look you, I'll teach you how to use the sling like nobody on the Island."

"Even Levercham?" I sat up to ask.

"Ah, she's not so good. I've beat her ever since we were in the Nursery."

"Not in the Competitions." They'd just been held, as they were every year at Samain to celebrate the harvest and show off Avalon's skill in the sword, the spear, and the sling.

"Well," Nimue said slowly. "I don't do very good then. The crowds —"

I covered my face with my hands.

"Argante, you're being as ugly about the Competitions as Cerridwen was about you and the shape-shifting. Come on, let's get your sling. I really am good and I can teach you."

There was something in Nimue's voice, a complicity and, perhaps, a plea for understanding. We went and got my sling.

Nimue and I practiced every moment we could find and she taught me so well that today I can hit a moving target at a hundred yards. But I still can't turn myself into a bird.

Not long afterward, Nimue came into the Nursery while we were listening to Cerridwen sing a marvelously blood-curdling story about Maeve, the Irish warrior queen. She called Faencha to her.

Faencha and I had come to Avalon in the same Gathering and spent our childhood together in the Nursery learning to walk and talk and not stick our hands in the fire. True, we fought from the time we shared the wet-nurse's teat, but we were the firmest of friends. Not that we were much alike, and certainly not to look at. I shot up quickly, too tall, too thin, and so fair that all summer my skin was as pink as the Sacred Bull's. Faencha was dark, an African with tawny eyes set against skin the rich brown of a young apple bough. She was, perhaps, the offspring of Roman Legionnaires who'd settled in Logres or Cornii. But her people must have been kings in their own faraway country, for her bearing, even in childhood, was more regal than I have seen in many a royal *rath*.

"We're going to fetch the cows," Nimue said. "Argante may come, too."

I remember the whole thing with a child's sense of wonder because it was a great honor and a bit of a surprise. Not many very young children were allowed to have do with the cattle. Eithne, the Chief Cattle Herder, didn't much care for youngsters and had convinced Lile, who was Lady then, that we somehow caused the milk cows to dry up. As Faencha and I left the circle around Cerridwen, I felt the others' envious eyes follow us.

I was terribly proud, then, as we set off for the High Pasture. Under a mellow autumn sun the oaks were going red-brown and the grass just beginning to lose its green sweetness. Faencha, self-contained as always, listened while I prattled on to Nimue about Nursery doings and tried unsuccessfully to sing the Maeve story. Nimue finished it for me, adding a triad in which Maeve is brought the bleeding head of her greatest enemy, Cuchulain, the Hound of Ulster. After she ended, she confided that when the Mother Choice came for her the following year, she hoped she would be called to be a Poet.

We were hardly out of sight of the City when we saw the cows already winding their way down from the High Pasture. "I don't think they need us to bring them in," I said and looked up at Nimue inquiringly.

19

One of her fair eyebrows shot up and she sighed. "They never do." She put her arms around our shoulders. "Let's count them and if they're all there, we can sit under that oak until they get down." She gestured to a big tree across the valley. "I'll sing you some more stories. Or we can practice slinging."

Nimue counted the cows. One was missing. "Old Broke Hoof, I'll bet. She's always wandering off by herself. Sure, I'll have to go look for her. You two stay here." She gave Faencha and me her warm smile and headed us toward the oak. But we wanted to go with her.

"I can find her faster. Your job will be to keep a watch on the rest. Especially that one there." She pointed up at the last cow. "That's Young Oona. Remember? You saw her born, so you're kind of responsible for her." Faencha and I both nodded, remembering the wonder and horror and delight of watching the wet little calf slip out of her red-coated mother.

Nimue moved off across the valley. After a few paces, she stopped and turned back to us. "Oh, and don't go back to the City. Everybody's pretty busy with Arthur right now. All right?" Faencha and I grinned at each other; it was a needless admonition. We didn't want to go back to the City. We were delighted to be on our own for once. And besides, this Arthur, whoever *he* was, held no interest for either of us.

For a while we watched Nimue walking up the hill, the cattle walking down. Then we went to play under the oak. The acorns would provide us with plenty of entertainment until Nimue got back. We arranged them into two armies, one English, the other British. We drew the British up into the strict Roman order we had seen on the Daughters' parade ground and were arguing about who would be cavalry and who infantry when we heard something in the grass behind us.

We looked around to find what appeared to be a large rabbit sitting upright on enormous hind feet. The creature stared at us for a moment, surprised, I supposed, to find someone sharing its ground. It twitched its brown nose a couple of times, then dropped on all fours. I expected it to go hopping off, but instead it calmly began to graze.

Faencha and I kept very still, interested in its business. After a while, it moved a little closer to us and we toward it. I waved Faencha back and plucked a few pieces of grass, then laid them down at arms' length, hoping the creature would come even closer. It stopped chewing at the dried stocks of sedge and eyed the grass. After a moment's hesitation, it took two little hops, gobbled up the grass, then looked at me expectantly. I set a few more pieces down and it ate them, too. Soon, I had the little animal eating from my hand.

This simple act of feeding a rabbit represented something of a triumph for me. Never before had any animal — dog, kitten, cow — voluntarily come at all close to me. Not that I mistreated them or feared them. I liked animals very much. But when I approached, say, one of the hounds, it would slink away as if I had beaten it. And I would wail in consternation and disappointment. I couldn't understand it. Nor could anyone else, and the whole business had become a bit of a Nursery scandal. Brian, the Horse Master, insisted I was afraid of the shaggy little ponies he tried to teach me to ride. Faencha suggested I squeezed the barn cats too hard when I finally managed to capture one. Among the *nainau* there were even dark whispers of a *geis* — a curse.

So, sitting there with that rabbit in the dappled fall sunshine, I felt very proud of myself and could hardly wait to show Nimue. Especially since after awhile the wonderful creature not only allowed me to give it grass, it let me stroke its soft brown fur. And then! And then, as Faencha squealed with delight, I gathered the courage to pick it up and hold it to me.

A shadow fell across us. The rabbit quivered in my arms and folded its ears alongside its head. I looked up, mouth open to exclaim my joy to Nimue.

No one was there. Faencha and I glanced at each other, then scanned the whole valley, but, except for the cows, who were by now meandering along the path toward home, we were alone. In the meadow, on the hills, there was no one. But distinctly I heard laughter. Laughter like the sound of a bell. And in the air was the smell of burnt cloves.

The rabbit struggled out of my arms and I went back to feeding it, Faencha now helping. Soon we had cropped all the grass close around, so we crawled a few feet away to gather more. The rabbit stayed where it was. We had gathered a goodly mound of grass when behind us I heard a sharp thud. I turned around.

The rabbit lay dying, a stone a little way from its bleeding head. In horror I scooped up the little creature.

"Drop that thing, Argante!" Nimue ran across the meadow, shouting at me. "Drop it right now!"

I looked down at the rabbit lying soft and warm in my arms.

Nimue raced up, white-faced. I stared at the sling in her hand. "Why did you kill it? It liked me. It came to me and let me feed it."

She knocked the rabbit from my arms. Until then I had been too stunned to cry, but when the creature fell at my feet, I began. And Faencha with me. "It's only a rabbit. And it liked me. No other animal ever did before."

I started to pick it up, but Nimue grabbed me and pulled me hard against her. "That thing's no rabbit, Argante. It's a hare."

A hare! A creature special to Annis, the Hag! And as such, cursed by the Mother. Forbidden to be touched. My sobs of sorrow turned to howls of fear. "Am *I* cursed now, Nimue? Will *I* be punished?"

Nimue held me close to her, running her hand over my head. After awhile she said, "It's all right, Argante. The hare's dead. And besides, you didn't know what it was, did you? You thought it was a rabbit. Both of you." She gathered Faencha to her, too. "I'm sure the Mother understands." She didn't *sound* sure, but I wanted to believe her.

Faencha and I snuggled closer into the comfort of her arms. We stood there under the oak tree for a long time, the dead hare stiffening beside us. Finally Nimue said in a thoughtful voice, "We'll leave the hare here for the kites to take care of. No one need know you — we — had anything to do with it."

I pulled my face away from her tunic and we

looked at each other. Then she took our hands and together the three of us walked toward the meadow where Old Broke Hoof was cropping daisies. None of us ever spoke of the matter again.

The next day a grey kitten followed me into the Nursery and took up residence on my bunk. The following afternoon I rode my first pony.

Dear Nimue. Always kind, always loving. But a trifle lacking in sense, even as Lady. Especially as Lady. That, though, is a story for another time.

Chapter Two

At eight we entered the Child Corps, where we learned the hard Roman discipline that some ancient Lady had decided would mold a better army than did the old Celtic methods. An old woman-song tells us she learned from Boudica's rising against the Romans that courage and ferocity are not enough. Three hundred Daughters died with the Druids in Anglesey during that war. And when the remnants of our army joined the Brigantes in the south, so weak was their discipline, and so great their grief, that they gave way to battle madness. It was the

Daughters of Avalon who hacked off the breasts of the Roman women as they fled from London.

The Lady would have no more of it. She hired Legionnaires — cruel men, but the finest soldiers in all the world — to reform our military. And though they charged an enormous price in cattle and gold, from that time on the Daughters have employed their ways.

That she was entirely correct can be verified through the briefest recollection of any British army before the coming of Arthur Pendragon. Or, should I say, before Morgant the Merlin Falcon. The British clans had gone back to the old ways, all foot soldiers and hill-forts. And the English won, regularly. But Morgant convinced Arthur to reintroduce Roman tactics. It was Morgant, Arthur's Avalon-trained sister, who made the clans understand the infantry wedge and the cavalry wing. Then came victory at Badon. And twenty years of peace. But the British follow Arthur no more. Well, these kinds who so devoutly bow their knees to the Christian god will soon be on their knees before English chiefs.

There were seven of us in my group by then. New children had joined us when we entered the Child Corps: the womb-children of the Island and the fosterlings.

Some Island women choose to bring forth children of their own, even if their soul-friends are female. If no permanent bond exists between the woman and man — and such a bond is rare on Avalon — the woman simply seeks out a man in the dark of the moon and conceives.

We Gatherlings had seen the womb-children before, peeking shyly from behind their mothers' legs at Samain or, sometimes, clutching their tunics in the market. Bog-babies we called them in the conviction that they lacked our City polish, stuck off as they were in herding villages or timber stations. Why, it was common knowledge that when they first came to the Child Corps, they'd never even *seen* a bath, much less taken one.

We could feel superior to bog-babies. The fosterlings, though, were another matter. Each spring brought carraghs full of them, arrogant young things in the torques and tartans of the clans they would one day rule. They spent the first few weeks fighting out their hereditary differences, then turned on us. They had better sense than to harm or insult us directly. We were, after all, the children of the Goddess. But they found ways to let us know that to them, princes of the blood all, we were just so much scrub stock.

The girls among them came from Ireland where military service is required of aristocratic women, and from those British and Gaulish clans where the Celtic Laws were still honored and women, therefore, accounted equal. Sometimes more than equal. A few would rule when their fathers died, the electors of their tribes Goddess-sworn to accept the first-born daughter of a king without sons. Some were of matriarchal clans that had always been ruled by women. Others had been born with exceptional talents that Avalon would hone. Marcail Blue Harp, for instance, had shown herself to be a poet of splendid perception. The Picts, though, whatever their talents in metalworking, have little tradition of song. And so Marcail was sent to Avalon.

It was as a fosterling on Avalon that Morgant

the Merlin Falcon got her military training. And probably her magic, too. Where she got her genius, I cannot say. Suffice that with it she quelled the English.

The girls from royal houses were haughty, and the talented were condescending. But those who, like Elin, were both! For them, we Islanders barely existed. That is why, I used to say to Elin, we got along so poorly when she was on Avalon. And she would say, "Argante, the truth is, you Islanders cared only for each other. You thought mainlanders far less interesting than even your pigs. Besides, you were a snot."

Ostensibly, Elin came to Avalon to study with the Healers — and never misunderstand me, Elin was a good physician, learned and diligent. But it wasn't the healed human being she was interested in; it was the adventure of the healing. Any adventure, I think, was the same: healing, battle, love. She'd discovered the adventure of cure the winter she was seven when a peasant boy broke through the ice in the pond that watered her father's castle. He was pulled out eventually, quite dead. But he was Elin's friend and, as many people do, she mourned with anger instead of tears. In her fury, she kicked him as he lay blue and still beside the pond, then fell on him and pounded on his chest. When his mother pushed her way through the crowd of bondsmen on the bank, she found the boy vomiting into the snow with Elin giggling beside him.

When Elin first arrived in Avalon, she didn't live with the Corps in the barracks, but out in the

House of Healing with the Mother-chosen Healers of Avalon and one or two mainland children who also seemed to have a special gift for curing the sick.

At that time, the House of Healing was little more than a cold, isolated rock warren. So we could understand this tall, quiet mainlander coming often to sit on the parade ground wall and watch the Corps train in the sunshine. What we didn't understand was that, when one of us stumbled over our long shields (they're not easy to use) or muffed a spear throw, she laughed. Not chuckled, actually laughed. Out loud.

One day, Con, the sword prefect, had enough of this arrogance. "Here," she said, shoving a wooden practice sword in the girl's hand. "We're all wanting to see what you'd do if you had a *real* job."

In a smooth, sweeping motion, Elin cracked the sword butt across the point of Con's chin. Con went down like a butchered ox. The Child Corps was impressed. When she came to, so was Con. To our surprise, she invited Elin to train with the rest of the Corps.

Gatherlings, bog-babies, and fosterlings. The Corps prefects, Daughters whose lives were spent training the young, had their hands full molding us into comrades. But they did, in the way of armies everywhere — by making us hate them more than we did each other. Short rations, forced marches, the thousand other great and small humiliations that children and soldiers are natural heirs to, all these soon enough made of us a hard little fist. We were no longer Argante, Faencha, and Branwen of Avalon; no longer Elin of Calchvynydd, Niall ui Niall,

Cadwallon ab Gwynedd, and Medraut of Logres. We were VI Section, plain, simple, and so much so that a parade ground shout of "Fall in, Six Section" can still bring me to momentary attention.

Three years after Elin joined us, another great event occurred in my life: the English invaded Avalon. Only that once in my childhood did I see the English. In those days, after Arthur forced the Peace of Radon, we didn't send a cohort of Daughters to their deaths against them each spring. (Deirdre — and she is not alone — believes the English are nothing less than Annis's Grey Host. Preposterous! Annis and the Grey Ones can assume many forms, it's true, but there is no use fearing the English more than they deserve.)

An English war party, bored perhaps by peace and prosperity, came out of a winter storm, taking Avalon by surprise. Within an hour of their landing, our defenses broke down; they were in the Crystal City before nightfall. They were fine warriors, smart and brave, but the Daughters at last pinned the main force down in the Lady Hall itself.

Naturally, in any battle within a city's walls there is bound to be a good bit of property damage. But over and above that, when the English realized they were defeated, their chieftain ordered his men to smash instead of fight. It was both silly and suicidal. Lile would surely have freed any prisoners, sent them back to Suth Seaxe in their own pointed keels. But no. Even after she made that offer, the chieftain went ahead and tried to destroy the Hall. He very nearly succeeded, too. He and his men rampaged through the living quarters and the indoor gardens. The Daughters caught them just as they finished demolishing the Mother's Crystal Shrine.

I was too young to fight, of course. In that, my first battle, I was a mere water-carrier. I stood with Faencha on the Hall Gate and watched the Daughters pour over the broken garden walls, surrounding the English chief and what remained of his personal contingent. When they finally threw down their swords, Lile bade them get on their knees. She said something to them I couldn't hear. Perhaps she told them to offer what prayers they could to their gods. She called for water and Meara, her soul-friend, brought it to her in a large silver basin. Lile washed her hands and put on a clean scarlet robe, which Meara also brought. Then she touched the Lady-mark on her cheek and picked up the sword named Silver Wheel, a long, Celtic sword, rather blunt at its ends, but wondrous sharp. It was the Lady's sword, bestowed on her at her Lady-making. It hangs beside me now.

Lile moved along the kneeling row of English much like a farmer moves across a field of grain. The sword wheeled through the still air, crunched through the living bone. Again and again. The heads dropped cleanly from the bodies — Lile was a big, strong woman — but she was soon covered in blood as the Englishmen's bodies flopped through the crystal shards and over the limestone rubble of the wall. When only the chieftain remained alive, she handed the Silver Wheel to Meara and unsheathed her short, Spanish sword, the kind with which Rome conquered the world.

The silence of the Daughters allowed me to hear

her words. "Them, I have sent to their gods with honor, and quickly, for they were but your instruments."

The Englishman snarled a reply in his own language and spat at her feet.

"You, I will slice up. Slowly," Lile told him. And she did — beginning with his balls.

All that winter, English heads decorated the City's gates and fed the ravens.

For several years before we rebuilt the Hall, it looked like the grey *dun* of any mainland king. But finally the glass panels were back in place and Avalon once again deserved to be called the Glass Isle. Lile declared a feast and, though it was nearly harvest, all the Island drifted into the City. The Child Corps was given special dispensation from its duties and allowed to flee the rock and splintery pine of the barracks, cold even in winter. The news was hardly out of Con's mouth before we rushed off to climb the big camellia trees and swing from the vines that covered the Lady Garden's west wall.

When we tired of that, we went to the smithies to stare as the iron bars were burned and battered till they became the weapons of war. We hoped to see steel being worked. Vainly, of course, since steel is used only for swords of High Kinds and Great Clan-Mothers. Otherwise, it's kept hidden away well below ground. We had only been allowed to see its making when we were introduced to the other Mysteries of the Goddess — during that same ceremony in which, under a mother-of-pearl moon, we learned our true names and watched mold and herb and horn mixed to form the poultice that would cure the wounds of mainland warriors.

The Smiths finally grew weary of us and threatened to set us to work pumping the big bellows, so we ran off to the stables where we were always welcome, to learn about the Lady Line and listen to Brian the Horse Master's richly inventive oaths. It was Niall's idea, naturally; he spent every free moment with Brian. To his great benefit, I might add: after he became the Ui Niall, his horses were known as the finest in Ireland and his mouth the filthiest.

"Let's go get some cider," Elin suggested when it looked as if Brian might be about to ask us to help with the mucking out. And away we went, leaving Niall to perfect his vocabulary.

"We'll bring you a flagon, Niall," Faencha called over her shoulder.

"I'd sooner swill up the privy of the Morrigan," he yelled back. Niall, that rarest of Celts, cared nothing for drink.

When we reached the parade ground, where the cider barrels had been brought, we found it full of Islanders drinking the Lady's cider and complaining, as country folk will, about the weather. There were mainlanders, too — Arthur's men. They sat in their great circle, hairy knees sticking out of Roman tunics, chests emblazoned with the Red Dragon, loudly drunk, but handsome behind their fierce, heavy mustaches. When I was a very young child, I thought they were gods. In a way, I suppose they were.

I envied my Corpsmates who'd been chosen to stand behind them as their shieldbearers. Our own Branwen was there, I remember, and Medraut, Lot of Orkney's son. (Rumor had it that Medraut was, in fact, Arthur's bastard — and by his own sister, Margawse. Myself, I've never doubted the story; the Pendragon blood ran far too thick in that one.)

The Lady and the Nine were drawn up in a circle that included Morgant the Merlin Falcon and Nimue. Lile, more relaxed than I'd ever seen her, leaned against a wall, skirt pulled up to her thighs, round face red with laughter as Morgant, Arthur's other sister, finished one of her boisterous, and scandalous, stories about the court at Camelot. When we walked by them, Faencha poked me and said, "See, Morgant's got her hand on Nimue's knee. What'd I tell you?" It was true; she did. And Nimue was curling her finger through Morgant's grizzled, damp-looking hair. Faencha, like the rest of us, was beginning to take an intense interest in love affairs.

Seonaid, the Hall Cook, handed us little cups of cider. "One apiece and that's all. I ain't letting the whole Child Corps get drunk today. There's enough that is already. Look at them over there." She nodded toward a small crowd from the First Century, the oldest rank of the Child Corps. "Just because they're ready to leave Avalon come autumn, they think they can slop down enough cider to drown an army of English. First thing, they'll be puking all over themselves."

We decided to take our cider where we could watch the antics of the drunken First. They'd rolled a good-sized cider barrel over to a corner of the parade ground, well out of the immediate view of Lile. The barrel was empty now and they were tossing it around over their heads. From time to time, it would fall on someone, much to the merriment of the rest. Boann Big Nose lay crumpled

34

in the middle of her comrades, whether from having been hit by the barrel or from too much cider no one seemed to know or care. They would tend to her later.

One member of the First, though, stood aside from the game. He was Balin, called the Brute, a thick, dark lad, heir to half the cattle in the north of Britain. He had a reputation for having a quick fist and a slow mind.

"Look you, that barrel's heavy and Balin likes to show off how strong he is," Faencha whispered to Elin and me. "Wonder how come he's just standing around. I bet he's up to something."

"Balin doesn't have the brains to be up to anything without Medraut," I pointed out.

Medraut seemed to do Balin's thinking for him. He was younger than Balin, but they were so close that we used to call them the Drone and the Druid. Medraut did remind one of a Druid: his long greasy hair nearly covered his face. But he was handsome enough, in spite of his milky grey eyes and long, turned down nose. And he was clever enough to have once stolen the Chief Smith's hammer even as she stood watching him. But, at the moment, Medraut was on the other side of the Parade Ground holding one of Arthur's soldiers' Dragon Shield.

"Let's keep an eye on old Balin anyhow," Faencha said.

At first, Balin seemed to be doing nothing more than drinking cider and cheering his mates on, but as we watched him he fell further and further back into the crowd that had gathered around the First. Finally, we saw him slip away and saunter all too casually toward the gate. Once or twice, he glanced behind him. We quickly stuck our noses into our cider.

When he had disappeared, Faencha poked me and said, "Let's follow him."

"Sure, he's just gone to pee," I said.

"I don't think so. He'd have done it against the wall like boys do. And he had a funny look in his eye."

"You think all boys have a funny look in their eye," I reminded her. Faencha wasn't fond of boys, and the feeling, from what I could gather, was mutual. At least when we were children. When we were grown, it was altogether different. I have seen whole halls of men grow instantly silent when she came through the door, so striking a woman did she become.

But beautiful though Faencha was, she was not meek. And now she prodded me, along with Elin, into following Baïin. Cadwallon, nasty little slug that he was, wanted to stay on the Parade Ground to see if Boann was dead.

"You stay, too, Elin," I said. "If she's dead, you can raise her up." We had all heard the story of how Elin had come to find out she had hands that healed.

Elin took a step in my direction. "I'll show you dead," she said, fists coming up.

Faencha moved between us. "Stop it, for the Mother." And we did.

It was high summer then and hot. The cattle stood belly deep in the streams and the dogs lay panting behind rock walls. Sweat made rivulets down our half-naked little bodies as we crept, one by one, out of the City and up the hill beyond. No wind stirred the apple trees in the orchards; the sky was without cloud, its pale blue marred only by a few hawks on the hunt.

Balin led us past the orchards, into the darkness of the Lady Forest. We crawled through the huge ferns that grew there, following the tunnel that Balin had already cut. Elin, always a lover of violence, drew her bone-handled knife.

"Put that away," hissed Faencha, taking charge again. "What do you think we're going to do? Bring his head back on a pole? We don't even know where he's going."

We continued to worm our way along for some time, the dark taste of fern and earth filling our mouths. Then the fern began to grow less dense until we came to the edge of a wide clearing. I stopped so abruptly that Elin, just behind me, almost crawled over my back.

"Look out, you clumsy bitch," she said.

I turned around and grabbed her by the shock of dark hair that fell over her face. "Don't you call me clumsy, mainlander. Or I'll cut your ears off and pin them to your ass." A hard swat from Faencha kept me from trying to carry out the threat.

"Hush, you two! Keep your fighting to the barracks," she ordered. "Get back amongst the trees and sit down. And listen, for a change."

We fell silent, and through the cool stillness we heard a kind of chant.

Faencha cocked her head and wrinkled her forehead in concentration, then whispered, "That's Latin."

We stared at each other, dumbfounded. We knew

a bit of Latin, of course; we weren't barbarians. But outside our sessions with Claudia, our Roman tutor, we rarely heard it used.

"I'm going to climb a tree and see what's going on," Elin announced, then shinnied a young fir. She was up there for such a long time that we finally had to shake the tree to get her to come down and quench our curiosity. "There's four or five of 'em," she whispered. "Balin and a couple of Arthur's men. And a woman, too. Fair, real pretty, but I don't know her." Elin was already developing her famous eye for women. "They're standing around some kind of altar and a man in grey is saying, I think, prayers."

We strained our ears to catch the chanted phrases, though what little we heard made no sense. "The lord be with . . . Blessed is he that comes in the name . . . This is my blood . . ."

These last words were interrupted by a crash of thunder so loud we jumped, terrified, to our feet. In the clearing, among a few saplings, we saw Balin, the woman, and the soldiers in a row facing the man in grey. He stood before a stone altar and held a metal cup above his head.

As he stood there, immobilized perhaps by the thunder, an eagle, its talons strong enough to carry away a half-grown lamb, snatched the cup from his hands. In almost the same instant, there was another roar of thunder and the clearing turned white and black and green again as a lightning bolt smashed the altar and flung the people around it to the ground.

My head rang from the noise and my nose was full of the smell. For a moment, the forest swayed around me. I shut my eyes — this was the way I had felt once when I'd hit a branch at full gallop. But I didn't fall and when I opened my eyes, the saplings that had dotted the clearing were gone. In their place stood Lile, Morgant, and Nimue.

Morgant and Nimue were poised over Balin and the soldiers, swords drawn. With her mottled hair and yellow eyes, Morgant looked like a hawk in the chicken coop as she grinned down at them. Meanwhile, Lile stood with her foot on the priest's neck. She was holding the metal cup. After she had peered into it for a while, she snorted, shook her head, and threw it, splattering, against what remained of the altar.

She took her foot off the man's neck, replacing it with Silver Wheel's point. "I'll not kill you as I should, Christian, for fouling this island with your grotesque rites. But if ever I find you on it again, the sea around Tintagel will run red with the blood of its monks." She prodded him up. "Now, come on. There's a carragh already waiting to take you back to the mainland."

With the help of Nimue and Morgant, though both of them were still a bit worse for drink, Lile herded the four Christians toward the City, Balin and the soldiers throwing stomach-curdling curses all the way. As the group came to where we were standing, Lile stopped. We could clearly see the black Lady-mark on her cheek, an oval capped by a crescent. "You there. Six Section, isn't it? Say nothing of this. I'll not have you bragging you flushed out a covey of Christ-ers with your own filthy little hands." After that, and noticing how full of dirt and leaves we really were — Lile loathed dirty children — we trailed behind, almost as abashed as the Christians themselves.

By then some fosterlings had come to see what all the commotion was about but ran when they saw Lile. All except Medraut. He stood smirking until Lile ordered him off.

As Faencha picked fern frond out of her hair, she said, "By the way, Elin, thought you said there was a woman."

"Sure, there was. Guess she got away on 'em."

I sniffed noisily. "You know, lightning leaves a good smell. Like spice." I put my arm around Elin. "Like you."

She hit me with an elbow chop to the gut that knocked me flat.

Chapter Three

So VI Section grew up healthy young animals, schooled in the arts of war and the hunt. But, as I've said, we weren't barbarians. We learned more from Rome than the turtle shell offense: we studied with Claudia, the old Roman tutor who Lile brought in to give us something to do with our free time besides play hurley. Claudia had come to the British mainland when her husband was hired as tutor to a colonial family who was determined it would remain Roman even while its estates were being overrun by English. I suspect she'd been rather glad to leave

Rome and its Visigoth conquerors even for the British wilderness, and so stayed on after her husband died, eventually coming into Avalon's employ.

Like her husband, and her father who had educated her, Claudia was a philosopher, a Skeptic who had very little use for our gods and, truth be known, for Avalon in general. But she remained for the oldest and simplest of reasons: the austere philosopher fell in love. At seventy. With Nessa, sweet, pretty, illiterate old Nessa. How we used to giggle as they passed the barracks on a warm summer evening, two elderly women holding hands and with eyes for nothing but each other.

No wonder Claudia disliked the girls of the Child Corps. No wonder she spent her time with the boys, making them learn Latin properly, while we girls were allowed to daydream our way through grammar and rhetoric. Personally, I thought that was grand. Let Medraut and Niall and Cadwallon spend summer afternoons grinding away at the subjunctive voice. I preferred listening to the bees and watching orange butterflies flit from flower to flower. As long as the girls of the Child Corps were able to read a bit of Virgil and parse a few verbs, Lile seemed satisfied that Claudia was earning her keep.

One afternoon not long after the incident with the Christians, Claudia dismissed the rest of the Section but bade Elin and me stay. "Sit down," she commanded, heavy white brows battling above her eyes. Elin and I glanced at each other, wondering what transgression we had committed to be kept behind while the rest went off to swim.

Claudia leaned back in her wicker chair and

glared at us. She was very old, past eighty, I think, for she could remember the third Valentinian, and he had reigned in Rome decades before. Her hands were covered with the brown spots of age and withered by rheumatism. Summer or winter, she wore a sheepskin cloak over her wool stola and covered her knees with a blanket.

"You two appear to have some intellect," she said in her rather stiff Celtic. "I think you may be able to learn Latin. I think you also may have the makings of philosophers."

It was a strange thing to say to two little girls who barely knew what philosophy was. And it must have come hard to her to find only two of her pupils for the life of the mind. Not until I was much older did I realize how important philosophy was to Claudia and what being a philosopher meant to her. At the time Claudia first spoke to us, Elin and I hardly paid any attention. We wanted to be at the lake with the others.

"You — the mainlander. What's your name? Elin? You seem to have thought about the universe. Oh, I know you probably think some god lives in that ash tree over there and that when you die, Arawn will come for you with a pack of red-eared white dogs. But you have a feeling for causation. You don't appear to stop with the old formula, 'It is thus it has been, and will be forever.' You ask questions. More so, I'm sorry to say, than most of the foolish fosterlings, who think of nothing but joining Arthur and killing Englishmen."

I stared at Elin. I'd never heard her speak of such things. Well, she *was* always in trouble for asking why certain animals were sacred, especially

43

pigs. And she could never resist wading in the sacred springs. But I hardly saw much in that and, besides, she certainly loved the Mother and sacrificed to her far more often than I did. Claudia's comments, though, must have gone to Elin's heart for she dug her toe in the dust and looked pleased.

"And you." Claudia pointed at me. "You have a knack for language and a feeling for history unusual for one so young. Oh, I don't mean the kind of history your barbaric poets throw into those long-winded, off-key stories they sing after supper when everyone is too drunk to know what they're saying — all genealogy and blood. I mean real history. You, I will have read Thucydides. In Greek. You, I will make a scholar."

"I don't want to be a scholar. I want to be a Warrior and —"

"Fat chance of that," Elin said with a sneer.

"Silence! You'll *be* whatever that gaggle of wild women want you to be. They'll send you out in the wilderness and let you starve for a week. And if you dream about a hammer, you'll be a Smith and if about a cow, they'll exile you to the Far Hills as a Herder for the rest of your life." She was talking about the Mother Choice, when the Goddess spins out the fabric of our lives. "They'll tell you your savage goddess chose it for you, and that'll be that except when they send you off to war from time to time."

She wiped her hand across her high, white forehead. "What I mean is what you'll be in your heads. They can turn you into witches or geese-girls or generals." She looked at Elin. "Or queens, for that matter. You can earn your mead making pottery or

44

killing English. That's got nothing to do with what you are in your minds. Now, go and think. Do you want to understand what you see or do you want to go on believing all kinds of disgusting nonsense, like — like if you cut off someone's head —" Her thin old lip curled. "Then, you've captured his soul."

She dismissed us with a wave of her gnarled hand. We walked away in silence, both of us shocked by the sacrilege of Claudia's words but flattered by her attention.

I thought about what Claudia had said and finally, without consulting Elin or anyone else, I went to her and told her I would like to learn about the world beyond the sea and the mainlands. In the end, Elin and I both studied with her.

Claudia became one of the great guides of my life. She would be amused, no doubt, to hear it. "A Roman? An *old* Roman?" she'd say. "There are gods, after all." But at the time I was hardly aware of her influence. Like all children that age, I was caught up with the discovery of my own uniqueness. I'd begun to think of myself as not only different from other Gatherlings, but superior to them. Nor did it take me long to determine why. I, and I alone, could know the bond of blood that fosterlings like Elin held so important — I had a family. A father. Or so I'd then convinced myself. And not just any family: the Pendragons! And not just any father: the mighty Arthur himself!

But it was not until the summer festival in the year I left the Child Corps that finally I came face to face with Arthur. That was the last summer of peace. Soon, Arthur would plunge the Celtic Realms into war once again.

Our summer festival occurs in mid-Elembiuos, the last of July, as the Romans would say. The Irish call the festival Lughnasa. On Avalon it is called the Mothertime, when the barns are filled with hay, the cows grown fat and sleek, the apple trees swollen with fruit. It is a time when the Realms gather and friendships are formed, alliances made.

As usual, the City was in a turmoil of preparation for weeks beforehand. The stone streets were scrubbed; the glass in the Lady Hall polished; the Child Corps drilled and re-drilled. Trumpeters composed new fanfares; Poets practiced songs long into the night; Weavers turned out endless yards of wool in the intricate Avalon pattern. Whoever was not employed elsewhere prepared for the feasting: wood and charcoal sat stack upon stack next to every kitchen, and wheat and beans filled every barn. Cattle packed the pens, ready for slaughter; deer carcasses hung from the trees by the dozen.

And the pigs were fattened. That's where Elin and I spent that exciting time — in the pigsties. One afternoon while we were slopping the brutes, Elin rebelled. "I wouldn't be here if my father were coming to the Mothertime this year." King Emlyn was engaged in some touchy diplomatic negotiations with a neighboring nation over water rights. "And, anyway, I fail to understand why we have to spend such a beautiful day up to our knees in manure. Just so these ugly things are fat enough for some filthy minor princeling to eat."

"Arthur will eat one," I said. "That'll make it worth it."

Elin put her bucket down and rolled her eyes at me. "Please don't bring Arthur up again. This pig muck stinks enough without having to think about that foul-smelling old man."

"Arthur's not old and he's not foul-smelling!"

"He's the smelliest, filthiest man I've ever seen. Last time he was here, he sat down to table with dried pigeon blood all over his hands. And chicken manure on his boots."

"All mainland warriors are dirty," I countered. "You should know that. They have the English to worry about and that's more important than a little dirt."

Elin paused a moment, then said, "*My* father's not dirty. And *you* should know that." She pushed aside an especially greedy young sow. "At least not when he's on Avalon. He goes to the baths immediately when he gets off the ship."

To that I had no answer. I'd only seen King Emlyn twice, but he'd seemed clean enough, sweet-smelling, too. And the truth was, I'd never seen Arthur at all. During his visits to the Lady, I was always conveniently away herding cows or out to sea with the fishing fleet.

We finished feeding the pigs and slogged back to the fence where we sat down on a tuft of dry ground. Elin plucked a blade of grass and put it between her front teeth. For a long time we sat, bored. Finally she said, "See that old black sow over there. She looks like Gwenhyfar."

I looked at the pig, her black hide streaked with mud. She most certainly didn't look like Gwenhyfar, but Elin often made that kind of remark because she cared for my mother no more than she did Arthur. Perhaps Gwenhyfar embarrassed her. The Queen was a loud, gaudy woman — she took full advantage of the royal right to wear more than six colors — and, sad to say, rather silly. Whenever she was on the Island, she would barge into the barracks to slobber kisses all over me while Elin and Faencha and the others giggled and pointed. Then she would hold me at arm's length and loudly announce that it was indeed Arthur I looked like — or Lancelot or Bedwyr or whatever man she remembered having lain with in her youth. Over the years I grew used to Gwenhyfar's foolishness, and to understand that her generosity was of spirit, too. But Elin thought her no better than any other slut who followed Arthur's army.

"Frankly, Argante, if Arthur's really your father and Gwenhyfar's your mother, you've got a mighty poor family." Elin spat out the piece of grass. "Even your aunt Morgant never pays you any attention. But then she never pays attention to anyone except Nimue."

There was no point in discussing family with a mainlander; they were all genealogy crazy. So I picked up Elin's game of identifying the pigs with people we knew. "Look at that one behind the rest of the trough. She's like Morgant. Always hovering in the background, directing."

"And as dirty, too. Why are even the women of your family so filthy?"

"How could they be lovers, she and Nimue?" In my youthful arrogance, I was sure that so young and handsome a woman as Nimue could not possibly find an "old thing" like Morgant attractive. (She *was* more Lile's contemporary than Nimue's.) "Morgant's so ugly," I said. "Hooked nose and grey-brown hair that always looks like wet feathers."

"And she spits when she talks. Speaking of ugly, see that white pig? She looks just like Kai."

The pigs, by now sated, lay taking the evening sun while shoats ran around in small herds, grunting and snuffling in the mud after whatever acorns they might find. Elin pointed to one of the bigger sows, who was watching us out of a tiny pink eye. I laughed, for the creature did bear a resemblance to Arthur's First Companion.

Elin particularly detested Kai. For one thing he liked to insult women. For another he was a Christian and Elin had pronounced Christianity a thoroughly disgusting religion after Claudia told her its followers ate the flesh of their god. She tossed a stone at the white pig. The beast wiggled and snorted a bit.

"See, Argante. She even sounds like Kai." Elin stood up and threw another rock at the sow.

I'd never thought tormenting pigs very wise, but it was one of Elin's favorite pastimes. She liked to see who would make it to the willow fence first, she or the sow. "Don't tease them," I said as Elin picked up her thorn stick. "It's dangerous. One of those things is going to catch you and root you right into the ground. Remember the time a pig ate Seamus? There wasn't anything left of him but his torque."

Elin paid no attention. Instead, she advanced on the nearest animal, a big red brute lying on her side with her back to us. She threw another rock, but the old beast didn't respond beyond a short grunt and a twitch of her ear. Of course, that didn't satisfy Elin. She marched up to the sow and laid her stick across the pig's back with a hard thwack.

Still no response. Elin pondered a moment,

looking at the clutch of stripey pink piglets asleep next to the sow. A slow smile crossed her face as she gave them a poke. That, as Elin knew it would, did it.

I've often wondered at how a creature that weighs fourteen stone can move so fast and through thick mud. The sow was on her feet before I had even registered the blow, and headed straight in my direction, screaming in anger, eyes blazing purple.

Have you ever heard a pig scream in anger? The banshees must have learned their sound from a pig. I have faced English in full battle gear bearing down on me with axes raised, bent on slicing me into thin strips. I have been in storms at sea, half-drowned and seasick in the bottom of a carragh tossed through waves higher than a house. I've almost frozen to death on a Scottish mountain. But I swear by the Mother, I've never been so frightened as while I watched that screaming red sow hurtle toward me. I can describe her now, down to the last dung-covered whisker on her nose.

I wasn't prepared for her charge because, after all, I hadn't struck her, hadn't bothered her or hers in any way. I was, in fact, still sitting down. But I suppose it was understandable that she would come for me because Elin was by then diving headfirst over the fence. To the sow, I was the obvious assailant and, better yet, a motionless target.

As I watched the charging pig — I was too terrified to move — Elin yelled, "Get up and run!" And I did. As fast as I could toward the fence. I could hear the sow behind me, chuffing and bellowing, gaining on me fast. Just as I came to the gate, which Elin held open, I tripped and fell — into a long muddy slide, but through the gate. It banged behind me and into the pig's snout.

As I lay breathless in the mud, Elin grabbed me by the tunic and hauled me to my feet. "Come on, run! Before we get caught!"

She pointed to the ridge, now enveloped in the evening mist. A woman stood there, looking down at us while her grey horse grazed beneath the apple trees. On the wind, I heard laughter like the sound of a bell.

I ran, dripping blood and pig manure. When I couldn't go any further, I dropped in a bean field and retched, noisily and painfully, while Elin laughed.

"Now I can believe you're Arthur's daughter," she said between chortles. "You're filthy, stinky, and bloody."

I was also furious. Because of her, I had been scared to death, would probably be on report, was covered with muck. And now she was again insulting my father. I got up, walked over to her, grabbed her by the hair and bloodied her nose. As a matter of fact, I broke it.

When we finally got up the nerve to go back to the City, I'd bathed in a stream and looked fairly decent. Elin had not only a very swollen face, but two black eyes to boot. I have to admit I was always glad her nose stayed crooked.

How splendid the Hall looked that summer. On its glass roofs, dancing colors, pinks and greens and blues, leaped in the sunlight as if the whole city were afire. On its peaks, the pennons of scores of nations rippled in the wind. It seemed as if all the world had come to Avalon. In fact, so many of the

51

mighty of the Celtic Realms came that I began to wonder who was left to watch the English. Merchant ships from the Mediterranean and carraghs, some carrying as many as fifty warriors, cast anchor in the Blue Bay. There were Roman triremes and Norse longboats. So many ships that they filled the bay like bobbing black birds. For the better part of a week, they landed, spilling people into the City.

When mainlanders had filled every house and inn and barracks, they spread their leather tents over the fields and meadows. The Daughters of Avalon crowded into the cider shops alongside richly tattooed Pictish warriors. Merchants from Spain stood at the street corners to listen to Irish gleemen baying out the deeds of Cuchulain and Maeve. From the parade ground came the shouts of soldiers at dice. In the Lady Hall, kings who regularly harried each other's cattle and enslaved each other's people laughed and feasted together, protected by the Lady's peace.

I found excuse after excuse to be at the dock, finally convincing Claudia to let Elin and me repeat our lessons seated on the rock quay. (Our punishment for the pig episode, Lile said, would come later and it would not relieve us from the study of Latin.) Among the first of the great ones we saw arrive was King Caw with nine or ten of his twenty-four sons. It was a good sign, for at last report, Caw's eldest son, Hueil, had declared blood-feud with Arthur. There Hueil was, though, with his kinsmen — a squat and ugly bunch, but smiling.

Some came in what seemed to be unlikely combinations. For instance, Agricola Longhand was aboard the same carragh as Sugyn ap Sugyn and

Aedan the Pict. They had been at war with each other only months before and spoke no common language. But when they hove to at quayside, it was obvious they had made their peace over an ale barrel. Sugyn was said to be able to drink up the sea, but Agricola and Aedan were also tankard-men of the first order. They were drunk when they arrived and drunk they stayed.

Not everyone came for the feasting only. A good many visitors brought horses with them to breed with the Lady Line. The sick and wounded came, of course, to be treated at the House of Healing. And there were merchants and craftsmen from a hundred nations, come to sell and trade and brag in the manner of such men everywhere. One or two mainland smiths, cleverer than most, came to ferret out the secret of making steel. They didn't find it, though they were willing to commit sacrilege for the knowledge.

One afternoon a day or two before the festival's main event, the Mother-feast, there arrived the sea-monster prowed ship of Lot, King of the Orkneys. With him were his younger boys, Gaheris and Gareth; his older sons, Agravaine and Gwalchmei, would arrive with Arthur's Companions. Medraut, Lot's middle son, was, of course, a member of VI Section.

Also with Lot were his wife, Margawse — she was Arthur's sister — and their grown daughter, Clarisant.

Along with Elin and Claudia, I watched the two women closely as they disembarked. My kinswomen, or so I believed. They looked much alike, short and plump — fat, really — with massive bosoms. Their black hair, pulled into identical pigtails, was streaked with white. I was disappointed.

"They don't look much like sorceresses," I said to Elin when she had finished a passage from Cicero.

She looked up from the vellum just as the royal family was about to begin its progress toward the Lady Hall. "You mean those two dumpy little women are the terrible witches you talk so much about? They look like onion sacks with handles. And listen to them. Self-important sows." Margawse and Clarisant were arguing about who would take precedence on the way to the Hall. "On the mainlands, you know, Margawse shows off by turning herself into a bird," Elin continued, still unimpressed by my family. "And then lets those poor ignorant oafs think it's something only she can do. They even call her Margawse the Fay." With a dismissive shrug, she went back to Cicero.

Lot settled the women's quarrel by the simple expedient of taking them by the arms and pulling them alongside him as he crossed the quay. We could hear them squawking in pain and anger all the way up the Hall Hill.

"Do you think they're sorceresses, Claudia?" I asked.

The old philosopher leaned back in the wicker chair she had made Faencha and me carry down to the quay. "Does it appear to me that they are?" she said in Latin. Then, "Margawse, no. She fancies herself a woman of learning, but I assure you, she's ignorant as a stone and about as interesting. Margawse's only a muddler and meddler in things she doesn't understand. But Clarisant may be something else again. She's in league, they say, with Annis."

Annis. The Blue Hag. Annis, Queen of the Wastelands, a mysterious country up north of the Picts. Said to be the most powerful sorceress in all the world. Said to command a corps of warriors, the Grey Host, who were neither dead nor alive. Said to drink the blood of babies. Said to . . . oh, all kinds of things were said. I had never seen her, though she had sometimes been to the Island.

"Do you think she'll come to the Mother-feast, Claudia?" Elin asked excitedly. Annis, at least, interested her.

"You take altogether too much interest in the sinister, little girl. Yes, Annis will be at the feast. In fact, she's already on Avalon."

Elin and I stared at each other incredulously. When had she come? How had we missed so important a personage?

"She arrived just after those three drunken louts who amused you so yesterday. I think you were too busy counting the Pict's tattoos to take much notice," Claudia said, adjusting her stola.

I vaguely recalled a carragh pulling in while Aedan and Sugyn and Agricola rolled about on the quay. A fair-haired woman had gotten out, followed by a small contingent of elderly warriors. She had made no impression on me.

"But she's the Lady's enemy. Why is she invited to Avalon?" I asked.

Claudia fingered the fine wool of her shawl. "I've no idea what goes on in your Lady's labyrinthine mind, but I rather imagine she had no choice. Not to invite Annis — she is, after all, a mighty queen — would have been an insult and a dangerous one. She could inflame the whole north of Britain against Arthur, for one thing. And if Lile believes, as I'm told she does, that Annis is somehow akin to your goddess . . . well . . ."

Elin and I glanced at each other. Neither of us believed for a moment that the blonde woman we'd seen on the quay was in any way related to the Mother, but we very much wanted to find a way to get another look at this wicked person. Perhaps tomorrow at the feast. We grinned, for once in agreement.

Claudia leaned forward and pointed a finger at us. "There is fascination in evil, little girls." She spoke in Celtic now. "And this woman, Annis, is beautiful. But I advise you to stay away from her. She serves some dark cause of her own —" Her voice trailed off and she stared out across the bay.

We saw that Claudia was troubled. She meant to warn us against Annis, against the attraction of evil, but her skeptic, philosopher's mind had no words to grapple with what was beyond reason. She was reduced to the weary, worried mutterings of an old woman. She turned to us, mouth open to speak again. Instead, she hoisted herself out of the chair and scooped up the rolls of books. "Come," she said. "It's time we went home to supper."

Chapter Four

On the morning of the Mother-feast, Arthur and his Companions arrived. They went first to the Crystal Shrine to sacrifice — Arthur was still in his pious period. It was there I first saw him, a hairy bear of a man mumbling prayers in his Logres-accented voice, pigeon blood dripping from his hands. His eyes, I might say here, were not really so much the iron grey his enemies speak of, but that grey which shifts colors depending on the light. There, in the glitter of the shrine, they were a soft bluish shade. Later, at the parade ground, they were almost green. But whatever color they happened to be, they were always intense. It was as if there were a bright light behind them, a beacon somewhere in his head that cast its beam out through his eyes. I think it must have been his eyes that made men follow him even more than his generosity or his courage.

And physically brave he was. I need not attest to that. But he was not morally brave. I think that is why he never recognized his children, bastard or female as they were. That is what kept him from confronting Grenhyfar and Lancelot with their adultery. It is what caused him to let the murder of Lile go unavenged and to allow the best of his Companions to sacrifice themselves in the pursuit of the Cauldron — what Christians are beginning to call the Grail.

That I got so close a look at Arthur was unusual, but the Lady's peace extends even to unwanted daughters (if such I am) and I was permitted to take my place in the Child Corps. Well, not quite my place. The Corps was drawn up in Roman formation, but even though at thirteen I was in the First Century and a standard bearer, I was assigned to the last rank, among the youngest. "You will serve as junior prefect for the little ones. They like you and they'll mind you," Branwen, then Chief Centurion of the Child Corps, said, avoiding my eyes.

"What does Lile think I'll do? Prostrate myself at Arthur's feet?" I asked her.

Branwen pulled at her curly blonde hair and looked so uncomfortable that I hushed. It was not her fault I was once again being hidden away.

After Arthur made obeisance to the Mother at the Shrine — and wiped his blood-stained hands on his tunic — Lile invited him to review the Child Corps. She doubtless thought he would take a cursory look, tell us what a fine lot we were, and hurry off to the Hall for some good Island cider. Instead, he spent well over an hour with us. With Lile in tow, he walked along all eight ranks, sometimes examining a weapon or straightening a strap. Now and then he would ask a name, particularly of the fosterlings. I could hear his big delighted laugh as he recognized the son or nephew of an acquaintance. When they got to the seventh rank, Lile began to whisper to him and gesture toward the Lady Hall. He shrugged her off. She turned and gave me a hard stare.

It was not necessary for her to worry, for as I stood at parade rest that long time, I had formed a vision of how it would be when Arthur finally came. Because I was flanked by children who barely came to my waist, a tall weed in an otherwise uniform garden, he could not help but notice me. When he did, I imagined, he would gaze long at me, then turn to Lile and say, "Who is this wonder child with the future warrior already marked on her?" And Lile would answer, reluctantly, "Do you not recognize her, Arthur?" He would take a long, a slow look. Then a slight smile and finally his bellowing laugh as he grabbed me in his arms. "My girl, my child." He would pull me out of the formation and shout the parade ground to silence, saying, "This beautiful young woman is my daughter! Honor her as such, now and forever!" He would kiss me then, on both cheeks, and bid me sit next to him at the

Mother-feast and there feed me sweetmeats with his own hand.

It was a lovely dream. I nurtured it, rehearsed it through the whole of Arthur's review.

He spent rather a long time with the seventh rank; it seemed every child had to be spoken to. By the time he finally started down the last row, the entire Corps was rigid with suspense and a clammy sweat had formed beneath my leather tunic. I could feel my knees begin to shake. I promised myself I would stand straight and make him proud. He stopped to talk with Pwyll of Dyvyd, got down on his knees to adjust the strap on Aedan's little helmet. He dawdled over the Lyonesse twins.

Soon. It would be soon now. My knees shook even more. Next to me, he commented on Drust the Pict's fair skin. "Looks like they're not born blue after all, eh, Lile?" Then Arthur was in front of me, his square bulk so close I could hear him breathe.

He moved past without a glance.

The tension on the parade ground dissolved. Someone giggled and, two or three children down from me, Lile ruffled Rowena Greeneyes' hair, a gesture of affection so rare that Rowena still talks about it. I don't remember anything more until I found myself back in the barracks.

Arthur's review of the Child Corps was the end of my participation in the public portion of the festival. Elin and I weren't allowed to serve at the Mother-feast, our punishment for the pig incident. Or so Lile said. We both knew I was being kept away from Arthur, and Elin, poor dear, had to suffer, too, her royal blood notwithstanding. We were not, though, to escape bringing the food into the Hall.

Under Seonaid's watchful eye, we joined Rhiannon the Hound — in trouble as usual for her nasty tongue — in toting great haunches of venison, whole pigs, roast chickens, pheasant, partridge. This while Medraut, along with another lad whose name and offense I've forgotten, rolled in the barrels of cider, wine, and ale. Lile had contrived to hide Medraut, too. Better to insult the King of Orkney than to subject Arthur to any unpleasantness.

When we were done, Seonaid saw to it that we had good portions of salmon, both smoked and fresh. We added them to the oysters Medraut managed to snatch from overflowing bowls and felt well rewarded for our labors.

Seonaid was a good old soul and when she handed us our suppers, she told us to go up on the Hill of the Mother. "Out of the way so them grand folks won't have to be seeing the likes of you." But, as she well knew, where we could see them. We sat down on the newly clipped grass and, chewing on our salmon, the five of us watched the might and splendor of the Celtic Realms file into the Hall for the feast.

The procession was a noisy one. Drum flourishes and the wail of pipes vied with battle shouts from a hundred throats. The kings of Britain came first, splendid in their many-colored tartans, each king with his own shieldbearer and piper. I recognized one or two of the younger ones as Island fosterlings: Constantius of Dumnonia and Uchdryd Cross Beard. Uchdryd's red beard already hung to his chest; it would soon be of such length that people would claim he could toss it over the rafters of his mead hall. The others I did not know, except for Lot of

61

Orkney. Medraut clapped loudly when Lot went by, but gave me a little wink.

After the rulers of Britain came those of Gaul, then Ireland. At their head was MacErca, soon to be a high king like Arthur. Finally, came Arthur and his Companions. They were led by plump Kai, bearing the Red Dragon standard. He wore his usual condescending Christian smirk.

"Christ-er crud," Rhiannon the Hound muttered.

Gwenwynwyn of Carleon and Medraut's brother Gwalchmai, said to be Arthur's bravest soldiers, came next. They'd already had too much cider and were playfully cuffing each other with fists big as the venison haunches I'd just cut. Lancelot, a head taller than his comrades, followed with Bedwyr and Morgant the Merlin Falcon. And there were half a hundred more, including, I was surprised to see, Balin the Brute.

Arthur, a wide smile splitting his yellow beard, had Gwenhyfar by his side. The Hound and Elin barely managed to stifle their laughter when they saw her. I slunk down behind a clump of gorse in embarrassment. The queen looked as if she'd been dipped in a goldsmith's crucible, so crusted with jewelry was she. In her hair was a high comb of green gems and long gold disks hung from her ears. She wore a square silver neckpiece from which dangled a large topaz. Of Pictish design, I think — it was nearly hidden by ropes of braided gold. A big amethyst penannular held the Pendragon tartan sash to the bright red, sleeveless stola that she wore over a linen tunic of deep saffron. Jewels flashed from every finger and her wrists were heavy with cloissonné bracelets.

Beside her, Arthur, ever the one for knowing how to present himself, wore the simple leather uniform of a Roman private soldier. His Island-cast high king's sword hung at his side.

Medraut inspected Arthur as closely as I did, and for the same reason. "Our god-like father," he said with a sneer.

I'd always tried to avoid Medraut and the snare of his bitterness, so I made no reply. After awhile, he moved further up the hill to glower alone. But Medraut did have some cause for his torment. His mother, Margawse, had sent him to Avalon with a Gathering, as Gwenhyfar had sent me, to protect him from Arthur's anger. But hardly had the Gathering reached open sea when the carraghs were attacked by a black ship. Twenty-two children and four Gatherers went down with the boats. Only the seven-year-old Medraut, tied to a mast, survived. The Scottish fishermen who rescued him swore the black ship flew the Red Dragon standard.

Lile and the Nine came last. I gave a shout of surprise when I saw that Annis walked with them.

Was she all that I expected? If I thought she'd be surrounded by some kind of glowing corona, then of course she wasn't. But she was a striking woman, with eyes the blue of distant mountains and hair the color of pale Irish gold. Through her hair wove thick strands of ebony beads and she wore a feathered cloak. Swan and pelican, egret and cockatoo — white birds from the world over decorated its folds.

I wanted to go on looking at her, but just then Lile caught sight of the punishment detail sitting on the Hill and dispatched Eithne to shoo us back to the kitchen.

The day afterward there were competitions all morning — I took a first with my sling — and in the afternoon more feasting. This time, though, Elin and I were relieved of kitchen duty by two fosterlings who had helped themselves to too much ale at the Mother-feast and ended by spilling bean soup all over the Lady Lyonesse. So Elin and I were at loose ends. My hope that Arthur would recognize me as his daughter was by then gone and any plot to see Annis foiled by the fact that she had departed Avalon at first light.

We wandered out among the shops and stalls. They were no longer crowded but still doing a brisk business. At a Pictish silversmith's, Elin bought a small belt buckle. She paid with some old Roman coins she'd won from a couple of Cornish soldiers who'd been foolish enough to play dice with her. I haggled with the Pict over a looking glass, offering my knife in trade. I told him it was made by the same Smith who cast Arthur's steel sword. He told me children of the Goddess shouldn't lie.

Next, we stopped to watch a game of hurley between the King of Dyvyd's men and a group of assorted Irish. Elin proved to be such an enthusiastic supporter of Dyvyd that when the game was over, the team invited us to their pavilion. Elin, usually so aloof, immediately accepted the invitation. I suspected their goalie, a tough little blond, had caught her eye. On our way, our Section-mate, Cadwallon the Slug, came puffing up to us.

Here was someone almost as fascinated by Arthur as I was. To the point, in fact, that for the last few weeks it had seemed as if Cadwallon could think of little else. He was an ugly boy, so fair and puffy he reminded us of nothing so much as a white slug. Hence his unfortunate name. His personality, what there was to it, was also unfortunate. He shirked his duties whenever he could get away with it; toadied to his superiors; felt himself infinitely better than any female, including, I think, the Lady herself.

He also bullied anyone or anything smaller than he. Once, Faencha and I came upon him tormenting a hound pup, tossing the terrified little creature into the lake over and over until it was howling and half drowned. We watched him do it twice, then without a word to each other, leaped on him and dragged him into the lake where we held him under water until *he* was howling and half drowned. Of course, Cadwallon reported us, but fortunately Con let us off with a mild reprimand for fighting off duty. The Slug, though, was punished for being a tale-bearer as well as for molesting the dog. He was also ragged unmercifully in the boys' quarters for having been beaten up by two girls.

For weeks before the festival, the Slug had been in a delirium of excitement. And well he might. As heir to the throne of Glevissig, a Welsh land that had blood ties to the clans for the doubtful north, Cadwallon had been chosen to be one of Arthur's shieldbearers at the feast. It was a great honor, if a political one, and I envied him. But it had swelled the Slug's head almost to the size of his belly. He lorded over everybody and particularly rubbed it in to me, for he knew I would have traded almost anything for an hour next to Arthur. And it was to me that he had the audacity to come running with the tale of his meeting with Arthur.

It seemed that after the Mother-feast, Cadwallon

heard Arthur dismiss Kai and the rest of the Companions, saying he was tired and wished to be alone. So when the other guests had gone to their own quarters and dark and quiet lay over the Hall, Cadwallon left his guard post to sneak a look at Arthur's weapons. He crept along the passageway, taking care to stay in the shadows until he reached the king's door. After a brief glance over his shoulder, he lifted the latch and eased the door open. In the room he could hear only the even breathing of a man asleep. He slipped inside, crossed the pine floor to the small closet where Arthur had put his weapons. There, he lit a candle and spent a happy few minutes fondling the steel of the high king's sword.

"It was beautiful, Argante. Ever get a chance to see it up close?" He knew I hadn't. "It could kill ten English at one swipe, it's so big. But only the Pendragon knows how to use it. At the feast, when he held it up in the light, he was like Lug of the Battles himself."

Just as Cadwallon was ready to leave the armaments closet — he had already extinguished the candle — the door to Arthur's room opened. Bare feet crossed the floor. Cadwallon hesitated, then drew his knife, ready to protect the Pendragon. As he was about to leap out into the bedroom, he heard Arthur's laugh, which was followed by another. A woman's.

Cadwallon then spent rather a long time listening to the sounds of coupling. "Yelled like a cat in heat, she did. Told him it was the best —"

66

Elin caught my arm and reminded me that the Welsh were expecting us. But I wanted to hear more from Cadwallon.

Arthur fell asleep. Cadwallon could hear his contented snores. The woman, though, slid out of bed and made her way to the closet. Afraid, Cadwallon dived behind Arthur's Dragon Shield. The woman entered and picked up the steel sword. "She laughed, kind of soft, and said, 'Now you're mine and soon all Britain with you.'"

The sword still in her hand, she left the closet as quickly as she had entered. Cadwallon saw her gather her clothes and move toward the bedroom door. "Then Arthur woke up," he said and paused to assess our reaction.

I was appalled and fascinated. "Who would dare —"

"Annis."

"What a lie," Elin said. She gave me a disgusted look. "Let's go."

But I wasn't so sure Cadwallon was lying. He hadn't the imagination. I told him to continue.

"I thought the King would let out a roar and tell her to stop in her traces, but he didn't. He just asked her what she was doing. And she said, real calm, 'I'm taking this sword so its curse won't fall on you, Lord.'

"'Curse?' Arthur said. He sounded like he was still half asleep. 'There's not any curse on that thing,' he says. 'And you of all people should know it.' Then he told her not to try his patience, what did she *really* want — 'And not some witchery you've invented for the occasion.' He was getting mad. Boy, I wouldn't want to be around if Arthur got mad."

"So why didn't you leave?" Elin asked.

I shushed her quiet and Cadwallon continued. "She says, 'It's no witchery. I dreamt I saw blood running from this blade.' And not English blood, she tells him. The blood of Celts. Even his own. 'You may think what you like, Pendragon.' Real haughty, she talked. 'But that is why I take this sword — to throw it into the deepest part of the sea where no one can ever find it and it can never harm you.' She was standing in the middle of the room and the moon was out. She looked — she looked . . . um . . . like she was made out of silver."

Elin groaned.

"Arthur, he says, 'I think I'll keep my sword, but I'll hear more about your dreams. Later.' She went over to the bed and got back in. It was like before and afterwards Arthur said, 'Now tell me about this vision you saw as you slept in the cold of Scotland.' "

We waited, breath held, for more about the vision, but at that point in his story, Cadwallon lost its thread. He once again began to describe Arthur's weaponry. In exasperation, Elin said, "You've already told us about that. Now what about Annis and her dream?"

"I didn't hear that part. They were whispering or something."

"Oh, for the Mother! This is just like you, Slug. Start a big lie and then not be able to finish it. You better get Elcmar the Man Harp to give you some story-telling lessons. Come on, Argante. Let's go."

"I'm not lying," Cadwallon whined, afraid of

losing his audience. "It all happened, just like I said. Annis was there. Honest."

"We've got better to do than stand here listening to this drool," Elin said, starting away.

"Wait! I did hear some more. All of a sudden, Arthur jumped out of bed yelling about sacrilege. He was talking about her body and the Grey Host and them fighting together."

"Who? Her body and the Grey Host?" Elin asked, winking at me.

Cadwallon ignored her. "He said a lot about honor, too. And she said she wasn't talking about Arthur's army fighting alongside the Grey Host. And that anyway, the Grey Ones weren't anything. Something about the power they represented. Well, Arthur, he didn't like what she was saying and he called her a whore and told her to get out — 'And take your evil with you!' "

"Did she?" I asked.

"Well, later she did. But right then she told him the Mother had failed him and would again and she, Annis, that is, she could help him. Sure, that really made Arthur mad. He slung her right across the room, but old Annis, she's a noisy old bitch. She just kept talking. 'I could rid you of your problems with the pirates and the slavers.' And the northerners, too, she said. Then, if she did that, Arthur'd only have to worry about the English. All the time, Arthur was standing there naked, with his big hairy chest heaving up and down. Say, is his thing —"

"Just tell us what he said, please, Cadwallon," I interjected. "No one but you cares about his *thing*."

"*He* didn't say nothing. *She* says she can help him. By destroying the Island, which is cursed

69

anyhow." Cadwallon looked from Elin to me and back to Elin. "Do you think it is?"

"It's not! Now continue."

"Well, then she says something about all Britain being his. And Ireland and Amorica. And he says, 'In return for —?' " Once again Cadwallon trailed off.

"Well? What did Annis answer?"

Cadwallon pulled his ear and scratched his bottom. Then he said, without looking at us, "I tipped over the Dragon Shield."

Once again, Cadwallon got lost in his story, but from what Elin and I gathered, the rest went like this:

Arthur ran to the closet and yanked the boy from beneath the shield. "What are you doing here?" he yelled into the struggling Cadwallon's face. "Who are you?"

"I . . . I'm Cadwallon of Gwynedd. I —" The Slug sought an excuse for being there, found none and burst into tears.

"He's one of the Lady's spies," Annis said from the doorway.

"No, no, no spy," Cadwallon blubbered. "Sword. See your sword. Then she —" He began to howl and Arthur dropped him to the floor in disgust.

"Even if he's not a spy, he's heard too much," Annis said, putting on her yellow tunic. "He'll have to be dealt with."

Arthur looked down at the boy huddled and weeping on the floor. After a time, in a kind voice, he asked, "Did you come to see my sword up close? Is that it, lad?"

"Y . . . y . . . yes, Lord. I —"

"So you could tell your mates in the Child Corps

you touched it?" The King bent down and lifted the Slug to his feet. "Come then, Cadwallon, is it? Of Glevissig? Let's look at it together." Arthur lit a candle and led the boy into the bedroom. As he took his sword up from where it lay, he motioned for Annis to leave.

For almost an hour, the Slug and Arthur talked and examined his weapons. The boy left just before dawn, full of excitement and hardly able to wait to brag about his adventure.

"Have you told anyone else this story?" I asked.

Cadwallon stared at his left sandal and said he hadn't.

"Well, don't," I said, but I had a feeling that by nightfall Medraut, Niall, and the entire boys' barracks would have heard all about the Slug's adventure with the great man.

Perhaps, though, Elin and I were the only ones he told. That evening, Brian took his mares to the lake to water them. He found Cadwallon there, drowned.

Deirdre came in just a few moments ago with today's report.

She slurred the names of the dead, giggled once or twice, then, right in the middle, went into a crying fit. The silly old woman was drunk! I let her carry on for a while, but when it became obvious that short of using a poker I wasn't going to get her stopped, I called for the young guards to take her some place to sleep it off. The guards were a pair of seventeen-year-olds, one a Warrior and the other an

Armorer, pressed into emergency Hall service. On their return, they asked permission to speak to me.

Macha, the Warrior, her flame-blue eyes snapping, informed me, "The whole Island's drunk, Lady!"

"Those that aren't dead," I replied and there was no mistaking the girls' look of disgust.

Macha's a pretty little thing with light brown hair, a voluble youngster I could often hear chattering outside my door. The other one, Flann, is tall with dark red hair and a deep cleft in her chin. I think they are soul-friends.

"I mean all you have to do is look out the window, Lady, and you'll see what a pack of cowards we've got on Avalon," Macha raced on. "They're down on the quay climbing all over each other trying to find a ship or a carragh or, for all I know, a piece of board to take them off the Island. Day before yesterday, I saw the Sea-daughters actually have to fight to keep them away from the fleet!"

And two Sea-daughters had died in the fray. Afterward, I issued orders that they weren't to endanger their own lives if it came to that again. A somewhat tardy instruction. I should have foreseen something of the kind, especially after what had happened when I sent the fosterlings home.

"The way the miserable cowards clung to the gunwales of the fosterlings' carraghs!" Macha's voice was surprisingly deep and now it was battle-loud in her indignation. "They almost sank them."

Flann nodded, and added with a sneer, "The boys were right to hack their fingers off."

I started to explain that no one can measure another person's courage, but looking at the two of them — they fairly bristled with self-righteousness — I knew it would be breath wasted. So I waved them out of the room, then sat and wept. For Avalon. For me. For Elin.

Chapter Five

In the autumn following Cadwallon's death, we left the Child Corps. The mainlanders went home to their distant *raths* and the families they'd almost forgotten. Many, Elin included, were to join Arthur in the spring and Niall would marry a king's daughter who would cost many horses. They took with them the fine, Island-cast swords that they were given at our mustering out ceremony.

We Islanders were assigned duties outside the City until spring, when we would go on our Year Gathering. Branwen spent the winter in a northern garrison and Faencha disappeared into the forests. I went to Tref Briga, a cattle-herding village. The less said about that whole time, the better — it was a harsh winter and we had to sleep with the cows. When I got back to the City, I stayed in the baths for a week.

In May, shortly after Beltane, Fand, who was Chief Child Gatherer then, drew up the fourteen-year-olds in front of the barracks. The Year Gathering marks the end of childhood, so we stood solemn with self-importance as she and the other Gatherers inspected us, Nimue among them. When Nimue passed me, she winked.

Then Fand spoke of the mystery of the Gathering. "You're expecting great adventure and adventure you'll get," she said in her harsh voice. "But it'll not be the kind you can come back from every night and dream about in a warm bed. You'll sleep on the hard ground with only a bit of wool between you and the cold and the rain."

Fand squinted at us, her eyes watering in the sun; Gatherers are people of the night. "I see some of you are thinking you've slept on the ground before. And so you have, but not for three months running. And not after you've spent most of the night crawling up a mountain with a baby strapped to your back and it squawling in your ear and peeing on your shirt."

Next to me, Faencha giggled. I started to smirk, but brought myself up short and gave her a poke in the ribs. I didn't want to be left behind. Fand's temper was short and she'd been known to leave anyone who didn't at least *act* grown up.

"As you know, folk on the mainlands are in the

75

habit of murdering their children. Some of them — bondsmen and other poor people — just can't feed another mouth. Others already have too many children to find honor-price for when they marry. Then there are the ones whose babies have been born deformed or blind or maybe because of adultery or incest. For whatever reasons, they take the babies out to some isolated place and leave them to the wind and the wolves. What we do on the Gathering is find as many of the little ones as we can." She smiled slightly. "And make different arrangements for them."

Fand was a forbidding woman, remote and frightening. All Gatherers are. Even the dogs slink away from them. All Gatherers except Nimue. I still think the Mother made a mistake there. To be sure, Nimue was small like the rest, but she wasn't dark of face. Nor did she have that air of cold self-possession. Though honestly, I don't know how she avoided it: Gatherers see too much suffering.

"Some of the children we bring back here, especially the female ones. A good many of you came out of a mainland bog, as did I," Fand went on, plucking at the edging of her green Gatherer's robe. "Some children — the ones that aren't very strong — we exchange for other, healthier babies. And those we find too late, we have to put out of their misery on the spot."

A shudder went through me. Faencha's mouth dropped open and she clutched my elbow.

"Don't worry," Fand said. "No one will be asking you to kill a child. That is the business of the Gatherer regulars."

I looked at Nimue in horror. She was staring into the distance.

"But we don't hurt the babies if we can help it. We take the weak ones, who still have a chance, to houses where there are strong babies all warm in their cradles. And we exchange them for ones we can bring back to Avalon."

Before we had a chance to consider all this, she added, "Sometimes mainland folk notice they've got themselves a new baby and sometimes they don't. If they do, they say the new one's a changeling and blame the whole thing on the fairies." She laughed then and it was like a howl in the night.

Forbidding.

Later, she marched us off to the waiting carraghs that would take us to one of the mainlands. This was a summer Gathering — Year Gatherings always go in the best and easiest part of the year — and it was in southern Britain, not so far away. Only if one is chosen as a Gatherer regular can she have the supreme privilege of a winter among the Picts in the north of Scotland. I admire Gatherers greatly for their courage and decency in a cruel job. But in my heart, I've always been very glad that I'm far too tall to be one.

The bad winter had given way to an especially mild spring, so we were not always able to rely solely on sail, the sea was that calm. Instead, we rowed — for what seemed days and days and days. Fand had failed to tell us just *where* in Britain we were going. It turned out to be Suth Seaxe, a very long row indeed. But more important, Suth Seaxe was the land of the English.

"Grand," I grumbled when she told us. "We'll either die at the oars or the English'll do it for us."

Fand heard me. "You — Argante! Did I hear you say you want to take a close look at an English village? Good. I haven't seen one in some years. We can make a visit together."

At that, Faencha giggled.

"Ah, Faencha. You'd like to go, too? I do like girls who volunteer."

And so it was that, a few nights later, Faencha and I found ourselves with Fand and Nimue, stumbling around on a dark hill above an English village. We searched so many holes and crevices that my knees were scraped raw and my fingernails torn halfway to the quick. When we found nothing, I assumed we'd go back to our base-camp in the forest and try again the next night. But Fand wasn't satisfied.

"There's a baby here somewhere. I can smell it. Can't you, Nimue?" She lifted her nose into the still night air.

"I can," Nimue answered. "But that filth down there —" She nodded toward the village. "Gets in the way. Don't those people ever bathe?"

I sniffed the air, too. It smelled as sweet and clean as Avalon's.

"We'll have to call our friends, I'm afraid," Fand said, then threw back her head and gave a short hooting sound.

In a few minutes, from out of the silence and shadows, there appeared two lean, grey wolves. Their eyes, even under the thin moon, gleamed evilly and I could see their teeth, bared and brutal. They stood staring at us. Faencha and I hugged each other in pure terror.

"I apologize for these spineless kits," Fand said in the old language. "It's often a great burden, being a mother."

When Fand spoke, the wolves' expression — yes, *expression* — changed. They broke into what I swear were grins and sidled, loose-limbed, over to her. At her feet, first one, then the other, lay down and rolled on its back.

I looked wildly at Nimue for an explanation. "They're paying her homage," she whispered. "To them, Fand isn't a woman, she's a wolf. And she's their pack leader, too."

Even Faencha was struck dumb by that one and the two of us stood with our mouths open as Fand accepted the wolves' obeisance. Later, I asked Nimue if the wolves thought she was also one of them.

"They do. Just another of Fand's pack."

"What did they think Faencha and I were?"

Faencha snorted and said, "Who cares? As long as it wasn't supper."

When the wolves got up, they set out purposefully in the direction of the village. The English dogs must have sensed them, for as we grew nearer, they began to howl in the most awful fashion. I couldn't blame them, but I did think their ruckus might wake the people.

"It probably will," Nimue said. "But they'll decide it's *only* wolves." And sure enough, in a few minutes we heard the English quieting their dogs.

We followed a narrow cowpath down the steep hillside. Besides the occasional wails of the dogs, the only sound was the soft shuffle of our feet. In the valley below was a winding stream, which we waded into and followed until we were so close to the village that even I could smell the English — like moldy wool and rotten meat. We crouched low when we passed the village, hiding beneath the stream banks when we could and pausing now and then to watch the dark figures of their pickets and listen for sounds other than the rush of the water.

We waded on and on, all of us, wolves included, wet to our necks and shivering in the night air. The stream grew narrow and sluggish, then became little more than a trickle through a water meadow tucked between two steep hills. It was clogged with watercress, delicious tasting but hard to move in. The mud beneath it was soft and deep; our feet made sucking noises as we pulled them out.

The wolves stopped and one gave a low growl. Just ahead of them, the baby, a girl, lay naked in the mud. She was so pale and glassy-eyed, and so still, that I took her for dead. But Fand slogged through the cress and scooped her into a wool blanket. "Threw you out with the rest of the nightsoil, did they? Well, we'll just see about that." She shook the baby until breath came back into her. The child began to mew, then cry.

Fand came back to the dry patch where we were standing. "I think she'll be all right. I can hear her little heart pounding smooth. What she needs now is some honey-water." She handed the baby to Nimue and opened a leather flask which had hung on her belt with several other pouches. She bound a bit of pig bladder over its mouth and punched a small hole in it. Then, taking the child back, she urged her to take suck.

The baby refused the nipple.

"Maybe she's just too weak," Nimue suggested.

"Not this one. She'll eat. So much that when she's a woman, she'll be strong enough to break an oak bough in two. Won't you, my brawny one."

When the baby again refused to drink, Fand bent down and whispered into her ear. The baby let out a piercing yowl — and took the nipple.

A wisp of a smile passed over Fand's lips. "We'll call her Beitris Strongarm. She'll be needing the wet-nurse soon, so let's get on back to camp. Carry her, Faencha."

Faencha shot me a rather smug grin and took the baby. Then the four of us — the wolves had disappeared — started back to camp. We hadn't gone more than a few steps when Nimue stopped abruptly and sniffed the air. "There's another child out in that bog."

Fand sniffed, too. "Deep in it, though." She peered into the darkness. "Can't see signs of anyone having walked further than where we found this one."

I looked into the darkness. I couldn't see anything at all.

"Over there," Nimue pointed.

"I see now. Ah, there's a cry."

I had heard nothing.

Fand hesitated, then said, "We've no time now. It's almost dawn. Come." She started for the hill we were to climb so that we could make our way back through the thick woods at its top, far away from the English and their nervous, noisy dogs.

"I'd like to search for the child," Nimue said.

"Denied. Come."

"I'm going after that child."

Fand's head whipped around. She glared at Nimue again and said, "Come." Still Nimue didn't move.

Faencha and I glanced uneasily at each other. This kind of insubordination could get Nimue a year in the mines. Fand turned slowly around, her eyes never leaving Nimue's.

They stared at each other for a long time, then Fand said, "Faencha and I will take Strongarm back. Nimue and Argante will find the other infant. Come, girl." The two of them moved off, leaving me confused and a little scared in that cold, dark, wet place.

"Why —" I began.

"Because Fand is too old now to go that deep into the bog. She just can't manage anymore." She looked after Fand. "Poor old woman. See how the wetness has made her limp? And she can't even carry a baby very far. I think this may be her last Gathering."

"Won't you be in trouble?"

Nimue shrugged.

The night was almost over when we found the child, another girl. But this one seemed less sickly. She didn't need to be shaken so hard and she took the honey-water eagerly. As Nimue tucked her into her Gatherer's pouch, she whispered, "She looks like the other one. See?" She did, but then all babies looked alike to me. "Twins, maybe. Some people are afraid of them. They think the gods send them as a curse."

We started for the camp. We were almost to the top of the hill when the villagers attacked. They came at us out of the woods so suddenly that we were easily taken, before we had a chance to draw our weapons.

There were four of the English, three men and a boy. One, obviously their leader, was a giant, fully a foot and a half taller than the rest and almost a yard taller than Nimue. He grabbed her by the belt and shook her like a big terrier does a mink. The belt broke, though, and Nimue scrambled to her feet, the baby still secure on her back. She slashed out a kick to his knee that sent him rolling down the hill. I think she could have escaped them, had she not tried to retrieve the flasks that had fallen from her belt. As she reached for them, the boy knocked her down the hill, into the giant's waiting clutches.

As for me, although I'd been taught hand-foot combat, this was the first real violence I'd ever encountered. Oh, I'd been hurt in accidents, but no one had ever tried to rip my head off or deliberately break my arm. It hurt. Badly. And, of course, for the first time in my life, I was afraid *for* my life. I didn't resist very long.

Once they had us trussed up, they couldn't decide what to do with us, or the baby. One of the men obviously wanted to dispatch the child then and there. He tried to grab her from the giant's arms, but when he did the giant rapped him hard across the ear. According to Nimue, who understood their language, the problem was that they assumed the

83

child was hers but they didn't know who or what *she* was.

"The one who tried to kill the baby thinks we might be fairies and the giant thinks we're human but enemies," Nimue whispered. "The older man says whatever we are, fairy or mortal, we're worth some gold and they ought to take us back to their village."

He won.

In the village, we were thrown into a round, dirt-floored hovel that stank of English. It must have been a workshop of some kind; there was a little seat and what appeared to be footrests for a weaver. In the middle was a small hearth, cold now and likely to stay that way. I was still very wet and I started to cry. Nimue let me sob for a while, but when I took to wailing, she told me in no uncertain terms to be quiet, dry my eyes, and "Remember, Daughter of Avalon, who you are."

She had managed to save the flask of honey-water and now sat cross-legged in the dirt, dry-eyed, calmly feeding the baby. I stopped crying.

When she had sung the child into a somewhat fitful sleep, we began to talk of escape. The solution seemed obvious to me. "Turn yourself into a bird and fly to Fand. Then all of you can come get me and the baby."

Nimue picked at a long tear in her cloak. "I can't do that."

I thought I hadn't heard her, but she continued. "You see, Argante, Avalon's magic is . . . um . . . not effective in lands where the Mother isn't worshiped." She took a deep breath. "Every place has its own earth, its own magic. Our power comes from our earth, Avalon's earth. That's why we always carry a flask full of Island dirt with us. Mine got lost in the fight."

"Nobody gave me any flask full of dirt."

Nimue glanced away.

"Oh, I get it. I've no magic anyhow, anywhere. Is that it?"

"Argante, I can't explain why some people do and some don't." She shifted the baby to her other arm. "It's the Mother's way."

Once, seated in her little corner of the Lady Garden, Claudia and I had discussed Avalon's magic — I bemoaning, as usual, my inability to master even its simpler forms.

"Let me show you something," she had said. "Bring me a dozen or so roof tiles and a hammer."

When I had brought them, she arranged all but three into two columns. The extra ones she extended across the columns. Then she told me to take the hammer and try to break the three tiles. I couldn't, though on the second try I brought the hammer down from high above my head.

"Now watch this," she said, pushing me aside. With a sharp shout, that feeble old woman put her fist through the tiles as smoothly and easily as a clabberboard goes through buttermilk.

"Magic, do you think, girl?"

"I —"

"You don't know? Good. Maybe it's magic and maybe it's a simple knack I learned from one of my father's slaves when I was a girl. Maybe I can do it because I know how — and because I believe I can. It could be that the *atomi* in those tiles didn't part because Jupiter or your goddess or Apollo Belvidere made them, but because I did. With my fist and my brain and my confidence. Now, I'm not saying that there's no such thing as magic, only that there might be another explanation. Do you understand?"

I gazed down at the broken tiles. "I do," I said finally. But I didn't. And I guess I never have.

Certainly I didn't there in that English village — which just then was coming fully awake. It was noisier than it should be, I thought, so I peeked through a chink in the door. Everywhere stood clutches of spear handles and piles of smooth sling-stones; tall linden shields leaned against the village walls. Warriors stood shouting orders at churls — so they call their freemen — who were driving the stock and lugging the beehives out the gates and into the forest for safety. Other churls worked feverishly to strengthen the walls and the smithies clanged with the sound of sword-making.

"They're getting ready for war," I said and Nimue joined me at the door. We watched them for a long time, not saying anything. Not knowing what to say.

Finally, I left her and sat down on the little stool. "I'd rather not get caught up in their troubles," I said. "We've got enough of our own. Think we can dig our way out of here?" I asked, staring at the dirt floor.

"I don't," Nimue said, turning back to me. "But there *is* something we can do."

"What?"

"Call Morgant."

At that point, I thought she'd gone mad. Morgant was hundreds of miles away — at Camelot or on campaign on the other side of Britain. "And, anyway, how can you call Morgant when you can't call on the Mother?"

"Morgant and I are . . . sympathetic, shall we say. Our . . . sympathy goes beyond time and place. Beyond earth."

Well, Faencha and Elin, I thought, guess we now know whether or not Nimue and Morgant are lovers.

She closed her eyes and began to mutter Morgant's name, repeating it until it became a low murmur, like the buzzing of a swarm of gnats. It went on all afternoon, until the giant brought us our suppers of whey and day-old bread. He set the food down just inside the door and eyed us as warily as he might a pair of wildcats. Nimue left off her chant, smiled at him, and spoke in the English language. He gulped twice, then turned tail and ran.

"All I did was ask him to bring us some cow's milk for the baby. In the meantime, the whey will have to do, poor little tyke." She fed the child, looked worried, then returned to her chant.

I picked up the bowl of whey. It smelled like moldy wool and rotten meat, but I was a growing girl and probably would have eaten it even if it had been. When I finished, I took the baby and spread my cloak on the dirt floor. In a few minutes, lulled by Nimue's mutter, the child and I fell asleep.

I wonder now why our sympathy cannot call Elin to me. Even from Ireland. Or Calchvynydd. Or the Otherworld.

Chapter Six

It took Morgant two days to get there.

But even before her arrival, we'd been freed from the hut. At dawn the following morning, a bearded old man we'd never seen before came into the hut. He wore a tunic of dark blue wool over which he'd tossed a grey cloak fastened with an iron brooch of rather crude design. With him was a woman wearing a wide-sleeved grey dress and a sleeveless cloak. Its hood nearly hid her face. A boy of about my age lingered in the doorway. He, too, was hooded, but I could see his milky grey eyes and recognized him as the lad who had been in the group that captured us. For a moment, though, I thought he was Medraut of VI section.

The old man cleared his throat and spoke in a tone that, even without being able to understand the words, I could tell was an attempt to mollify. Nimue's lips twitched as he talked and she bit away a smile. When he finished, she gazed at him for a moment, then held up her hand to indicate that she wanted to speak to me before she answered him. "They think we're *waelcyrges*. And they're afraid they've displeased us."

"*Waelcyrges?* What's that?"

She explained that *waelcyrges* are the priestesses of their god of battles, called Odin. It seems the English believe that when they make war, the ones who will live and the ones who will die are chosen by lot. The *waelcyrges* cast these lots. Odin chooses his victims through the instrument of his priestesses."

"For the Mother," I cried. "Are the English truly that stupid?"

"And superstitious to boot. At any rate, these English have some neighbors they've been warring with off and on for years. With rather poor luck, I gather. But now, since they've got us — *waelcyrges,* that is — they think things will go better for them." She shrugged. "I see no other choice than to go along with them, for the time being at least. Besides, they want us to bathe and then they'll give us clean clothes and more comfortable quarters. This, by the way, is the headman. And his wife and son, no less."

I glanced at the English. They looked like three

hunting dogs, alert and anxious to do what was expected of them. I decided that the *waelcyrge* thing must be true. If they wanted to kill us or sell us into slavery, they wouldn't need a silly story like that.

"How do these priestesses of Odin act?" I asked. "I mean, how should I carry myself?"

"I haven't the faintest notion. But I don't think the English do either, so just follow my lead," Nimue said, and, drawing herself up to her full four and a half feet, swept majestically past the English. I followed, smacking my head on the lintel and stumbling over the doorstep.

From that time on, we were treated like the visiting royalty the English had convinced themselves we were. But they had no baths. We were asked to bathe in the horse trough. I didn't like the look of the green scum in its corners, but it was certainly better than nothing. When we'd done, the chief's wife wrapped the baby in warm wool, then she and the boy led us down the dirt road along which the village's daub and wattle houses stood.

The women and children had apparently fled — or been shooed — into their homes, for they were nowhere to be seen. From time to time, though, we could hear a few giggles, followed by the sound of a child being smacked.

"I bet they think they'll turn to stone or go blind or be struck by lightning if they look at us," I said as we walked by. Then I twisted my hand into a claw and thrust it toward a house. "Hannh!" I hissed.

Nimue grabbed me by the hair. "Don't be any more of a fool than you have to be, Argante. Our lives depend on the awe these people hold us in. And if you make fun of that awe or diminish it in any way, we are dead Daughters. People don't take kindly to having their beliefs trifled with."

She gave my hair an extra yank before she let go. We walked on and after awhile, I mumbled, "That's what Claudia says, too."

"Then it *must* be true." Her sarcasm was not lost on me.

The village was a fairly small one as these places go. Perhaps a hundred people lived in its ankle-deep mud. But I believe it was a place of some importance, for we were led to a complex separated from the rest of the village by a spiked palisade. Inside, surrounded by a few gabled wooden houses and huts, stood a smallish, rectangular hall. It, too, was wooden, but had elaborately decorated gable-posts and a shingled roof. The approach was gravel — I was glad to see that English chieftains didn't have to tramp around in the same mud as their churls — and the hall's double doors were fierce with carved dragons and other peculiar beasts. There was no royal apartment in it; the chief and his wife slept in one of the complex's detached houses. It was to one of these we went. And a barren little thing it was, too. Ill-lit, damp, meagerly furnished.

In exchange for our torn tunics, the chief's wife handed us twill dresses. They were a rather dismal grey, but handsomely woven in a half-diamond pattern — and clean. With her fair hair, Nimue looked like an English goddess should. I can't say how I looked, but I felt very uncomfortable. I'd never had on a long skirt before. On Avalon only grown women wear them and then only on feast days. But among the English even the tiniest little girls staggered beneath their weight.

The chief's son left us at the door. I was glad, because his eyes, strange but at the same time familiar, made me uneasy.

Now that we were in her house, the chief's wife pulled back her hood a little. English women seem never to remove their hoods completely. She was middle-aged, a lean, strong woman with a leathery face and greying blonde hair. She said something in a tone that made me rather reluctant to turn my back on her. Nimue explained that she had announced we would eat soon. She added, "I think we may be in some danger from this woman. She's a lot smarter than her menfolk."

"You mean she actually thinks it's odd that these warrior women would just be wandering around in the village woods, and carrying a baby?"

"Clever lady, eh? Anyway, we've got to convince her we are what the men want us to be."

"How? And what *do* they want us to be?"

"Choosers of the Slain, that's what *waelcyrge* means." Nimue broke into laughter. "These *waelcyrge*, it appears, are rather nasty. From the stories I've heard about them, it seems that the English see them as weavers. Only their looms are made from human guts and weighted with severed heads. The design they weave has a background of grey spears, which they fill in with a bloody weft. The English believe that's the way these women work out the fate of the warriors. The English are very high on fate."

Before I could decide whether or not Nimue was joking, the chief's wife ushered us outside where a trestle table was set with beef and beans. It looked good enough, but gave off that sickly English smell. This time even I could eat little of it, in part because as we sat on the green, the English churls and their women couldn't refrain from peering over the fence at us. Such an ugly people. They all look alike, you know, with those white moon faces and that colorless hair. And they're not very bright, either. They just stood there, grunting, fingers in either their mouths or their noses.

It was no wonder the baby got crankier and crankier, even though the chief's wife had provided a wet-nurse. Finally, she was squalling herself purple and no amount of feeding, changing, or cooing could stop her. Nimue declared the child wasn't sick and certainly she didn't sound it. The turns we took holding her became briefer and briefer, until we were passing her back and forth like a hurley ball.

The chief's wife, naturally, noticed all this and at last asked if she could take her. Nimue was a bit reluctant, but by that time we were both at the end of our patience, and besides, we didn't want to annoy the woman in any way.

She asked the baby's name and Nimue, assuming the Chief Child Gatherer's right to name, said, "Cailen." The woman picked up the screaming child and began to sing — a strange, tuneless, shrill thing. Cailen opened her bluish eyes wide for a moment, then fell straight to sleep.

"How'd she manage that, I wonder?" I asked Nimue.

"Hard to tell, especially in view of the fact that the song's some kind of battle hymn, all about blood, flames, and fate. These people are crazy with war."

And, sure, they were. All afternoon, from inside the hall, we could hear the chief's hearth-companions shouting their drunken battle-boasts. Toward evening, the chief, his son, and a little group of warriors came out. With them was a brindle-haired churl. When the group reached us, he prostrated himself in front of Nimue.

With a look of amused delight, she prodded him with her toe. "Get up, Morgant," she said in British. "I'm sure they're already convinced without further dramatics."

Morgant! I looked at the wiry little figure lying face down on the grass. It looked like a man, beard and all, and was dressed like all the other Englishmen — grubby tunic, frayed leather leggings. And he was surely as dirty. But when he — she — stood, I recognized the hooked nose and yellow eyes.

"Who do they think you are?" Nimue demanded.

"Their bee-man," Morgant answered. "He's taking a little nap out in the woods right now. In the meantime, he kindly gave me the loan of his clothes and a bit of his face. Nice, ain't it?"

Before Nimue could respond, Morgant turned to the chief and his men to converse in great seriousness. After much nodding and the usual English grunting, she said, again in British, "We'll be out of here by dark. Who's this?" she asked, gesturing toward me. When Nimue told her she looked blank for a moment, then grimaced. "Of all the shitty luck."

Nimue glanced at me and said quickly, "How do

you propose to get us out of here by dark, or any other time?"

"With a bee charm."

"I see."

"Now before you get your twat in a twist, let me explain."

Nimue crossed her arms. "Do that."

Morgant cleared her throat and said, "Look you, the English have 'em a charm they use to keep a swarm of bees from flying away. We do, too, of course."

"Thank you," Nimue commented, arms still crossed.

"And I got 'em persuaded it'll work on you. It goes this way: Me being the beeman, I takes some sand, I throws it under my right foot and then I says, 'I catch it under foot, I've found it. Earth can work against all creatures.' Then I throw sand over the bees whilst they're swarming and say, 'Sit you, victorious women, descend to earth. Never fly wild to the wood. Be you as mindful of my welfare as every man is of food and native land.' "

"Very interesting. And very effective with bees, I'm sure. But *what* about *us*?" Nimue bit out the question.

Morgant sighed. "I'm surprised at you, lover. It's pretty obvious. The whole charm — words and all — fits your situation. Which is why I picked a beeman to disguise myself as, 'course." She grinned smugly. "When I'm supposed to toss the sand on the bees — that is, on you — I substitute this —" From under her dirty cloak, she whipped out a blue leather pouch.

Nimue eyed it closely for a moment, then said,

"Island dirt. So instead of settling like good English bees should, we shift our shapes and fly away." One of her fair eyebrows shot up. She paused. "A bit elaborate, but it might just work."

" 'Course, it'll work. Wasn't it me moved the Dancing Stones to Salisbury Plain? Wasn't it me called down the lightning at Badon?" She spread her arms in an expansive Morgant gesture. "Have you ever known my magic to fail, then?"

"Well, there was the time —"

"As for Argante's . . . um . . . disability," Morgant broke in. "I'm sure this time she'll rise to the occasion."

It was Nimue's turn to grimace. I just bit my lip.

Morgant spoke to the chief, who had all the while hovered in the background, looking apprehensive. The man now nodded and grunted out a few words.

"Morgant told him she, that is, the beeman, and the *waelcyrges* appear to be sympathetic and that the bee charm will work," Nimue translated. "The chief says it better." She ran her hand through her hair. "I agree with the chief."

Morgant and the chief, with his son, wife, and warriors, then escorted us to the hall and through its big double doors. It was crowded with the chief's hearth-companions, who fell back as we moved across the stone floor to a raised platform at the far end. There the chief and his wife sat down behind a trestle-table and bade us take one of the benches that hung from the wall. The boy settled himself some place in the shadows behind the table.

Compared to the Lady Hall, the place was

cramped and ugly. Because there were no apartments in it, the chief's companions slept, ate, drank in this one bare, dark, smoky room. Add to that the badly preserved animal heads and skins tacked to the walls and it's no wonder the stink set me gagging.

"If you throw up now, *our* heads will be lining the rafters," Nimue whispered as she settled the baby on her lap. "Look, there's a dragonskin." She nodded toward a strip of what looked like the hide of an oversized and long-dead rat. It was dry and puckered and covered with a sinister blue-green mold.

The chief finally managed to quiet his men. It had taken a while, for these English warriors were drunker than any hall full of Irish. But at last they came to something like order and Morgant began her act. The chief's wife got up from the table and extended her hand to us, as if to introduce us to the hallmen. As we took the center of the platform, Morgant stepped forward and started her chant. She took out the blue pouch and tossed some of its contents under her right foot. "I catch it under foot —"

I could hear the men draw in their breaths. Even the drunkest of them, or at least those who could still stand, leaned forward in anticipation. Their fates, they believed, hung on this lowly churl's ability. "Earth can work against all creatures," Morgant continued.

She tossed the Island dirt over Nimue, the baby, and me. I shut my eyes, prepared to open them on Avalon. There was a tremendous clap of thunder.

Then silence. After a moment or so, I cautiously opened one eye. The three of them were no longer before me.

But I was still in the English meadhall.

The astonished English blinked away the acrid smoke Morgant's departure left behind and, for a long moment, were absolutely still. Then they went wild. They crashed up over the lip of the platform like an armored wave. Once again, I thought Arawn had come for me. But before they focused their fury, a strong arm was around my neck and I was being dragged out a back door.

Outside, my rescuer pulled me through the dusk toward the spiked palisade. We clambered over it. On the other side, the chief's hard-faced wife, she who had saved me, pointed toward the wooded hill that lay across the valley. The boy stood next to her, smiling, though the smile did not reach his milky eyes. Before I could turn and run, the woman pushed me against the fence and pinned my arms there. I could feel her clove-scented breath hot in my face.

"The time is not yet come," she said and laughed. Her laughter sounded like copper bells. Then she let me go and sent me into the fields with a hard crack to my behind. I was halfway up the hill before I realized she had spoken in Celtic.

The forest was thick and dark, but I crashed through it until I could no longer hear the rage of the village. The Englishwoman had held them off somehow — over my shoulder, through a fast-rising mist, I'd seen her pointing in the wrong direction. I fell behind an old log, where I stayed all night and into the next morning, when hunger and thirst at last won over fear. Then, after sucking up some ground-water, I wandered around for the rest of the morning — in circles, I imagine — until I happened into one of those patches of open ground even the darkest forest occasionally affords.

In the middle of it was a dragon.

Until I'd seen that dilapidated old skin in the English hall, I'd thought dragons were the products of mead-soaked imaginations or thirty-year-old memories. But here was a live one and right in front of me. Forty feet long, wide as a house, smelling of sulphur and burnt flesh. I was already thoroughly frightened, but even so I slipped behind an oak.

The beast lay beneath the overhanging trees, pine-filtered light dappling her body. She was licking her hide much as a cat does, slowly, sensuously. She even purred, a sound like a sword being pulled across a rasp. She must have been quite old, for long dark scars ran down her grey flanks and her tail had a kink in it. One ear was gone. She had no fresh wounds, but she groaned when she moved. Rheumatism, perhaps.

I watched her for a long time wishing I could attack her. A dragonskin would look fine mounted in the Lady Hall. Especially one provided by me. And oh, what a woman-song *that* would make. But there I was, unarmed, exhausted, half-starved, and alone. Best that I simply creep away before I found myself boiled alive in the hot steam of her breath or snapped in two by a flick of her tail.

As I turned to go, I heard the very slightest rustle. Then the dragon pounced — as a cat does on a mouse, catching me between her two front paws and pinning my arms to my side so I could hardly breathe. Her great jaws opened and the green tongue licked out. For the second time in a few hours, I prepared for death.

"Well, so now you've seen a dragon." She talked! And in the old language, the dialect of the ancient triads, though the sound of the words was different, somehow clearer than when Elcmar drilled us in that terribly difficult tongue.

Even now, I hesitate to tell about that dragon. No one has ever believed she talked. Everyone says it's a fairy tale. Everyone except Lile. When she heard the story, she pursed her lips so tight they turned white. Then she laughed and laughed and laughed.

"What do you think?" the dragon asked. "Am I everything you thought one of my kind would be?" She loosened her hold on me a bit and I found breath enough to speak.

"I . . . I didn't think there were any . . . any of your kind left."

"Well, as you can plainly see, there are. Nor am I the only one. But we are few and grow fewer every year. Men hunt us down, slaughter our young, destroy our breeding grounds. Drive us deeper into the wild, where we starve. All so their corn can grow and their cattle can graze with only wolves and wildcats and other puny creatures to worry them."

She let me go then and I staggered back against a tree, my knees like icy water. "I . . . I just escaped from some English. They had a dragonskin," I said, thinking as fast as I could. "But I'm a Celt. We don't hunt dragons."

"Hah! Celts *do* hunt us. But I tell you this, girl.

When we are gone, the Celtic Realms will go, too. When the last dragon is hauled out of his cave, hacked up, and carted back to some very brave Welsh or Logrish warrior's *dun,* that warrior will have spilled the last of the blood from which his race sprang. The cup will be empty. It will be only a matter of time before the English and the Christians will do what even mighty Rome could not."

She sat back on her haunches and curled her tail around her. "Nor can we be put in cages like crawling, garbage-eating tame bears for some drunken Irish brute to wrestle so that his manhood can be proved. You mind what I tell you. When the dragons die, the Mother will weep for her mortal children, too. Then will Avalon disappear beneath the sea."

She stopped and eyed me. "But enough. I spend too much time alone. I'm beginning to sound like a Christian hermit preaching to his cave." She laughed; it was a noisy grate. "Who are you? One of Fand's Year Gatherers from your age and your bad accent, I'd say. I think I know where your camp is and I haven't seen Fand in years. A good woman, she is."

The dragon rose. "Hop aboard," she said. I hesitated for a moment, then crawled up her tail to her wide back. And there I sat, stiff with fear and pride, when Fand and Faencha met us at the camp.

Today, leaving Deirdre behind, Macha, Flann and I drove an ox cart loaded with a tun of water out to the Healers' herb garden. The water came from the

Lady Hall's own spring, which somehow hasn't yet dried up, all praise to the Goddess. We went without Deirdre because the garden's not the place for her. The Healers permit only joyful conversation there, in the belief that plants not only hear human voices but understand words. An angry comment in April, they say, will cause the tender plants to wither in August. I cannot attest to the truth of this, but on the rare occasions — rare heretofore — when the Healers fail, they immediately point the finger of blame at some Daughter whose complaining voice was overheard, they declare, by the fleabane.

Therefore, the herb garden lies in a little valley well away from the City. Its cultivation is ordinarily done by the youngest Healers as their first lesson in the *materia medica* and the patient optimism of gardeners and physicians. Since only one young Healer can be spared for farm work just now, I had brought Flann and Macha to help her. Lara is her name, a tall rangy girl, black like Faencha.

Poor thing, she's lonesome all by herself out there and she began to chatter the moment we arrived. "First we'll water everything, then we'll pick the vervain," she said as she handed the two their sickles and wicker baskets. "That's for warding off the evil eye. And then the Hound's Tongue, for burns, bruises, and bowels. And then —"

I left them to that vast field, half of it already dead, row after row of chickweed, figwort, hyssop, mad dog weed, heartsease, lungwort, and who knows what else. Even the walls are stuffed with house leek, for ailments of the skin, I'm told, and ground ivy for those of the lung. Flann looked considerably annoyed when she realized she'd have to spend a long day there carrying a heavy basket and swinging an iron sickle. I didn't think it necessary to tell her she'd be coming back every day till the harvest was done. What harvest there would be.

I made my way to the Moon Garden, a garden within a garden. There grows the herb that brings us the Mother Dreams when we sleep on a pillow stuffed with its silvery, aromatic leaves. Ordinarily, the Chief Healer, and she alone, works in the Moon Garden. But, I thought as I unwrapped the steel implements, Fedelm is old and the two other Healers still alive at the House of Healing have no time to worry about the Mother Choice. The future of Avalon is my problem.

Chapter Seven

At our own Mother Choice, my worst fear came true. I dreamt about a cow, and thereby the Goddess called me to be one of Avalon's Herders. I won't go into details; nothing bores me more than the particulars of the Mother-dream, or any other dream, for that matter. Suffice to say that a week later I was back in Tref Briga, sleeping with the cattle. Only this time, I thought, it would be for life.

Before I left the City, I visited Claudia in her rooms. She at least, would understand my disappointment.

"A Herder, eh, little girl? Better than the mines. Or the forges. Poor Faencha will be deaf in a few years and her face like old leather from all the pounding and smoke," she said as she knocked some grit out of her sandal.

"But Faencha *wanted* to be a Swordsmith. I wanted to be a Warrior. Like Branwen did and now she *is* a Warrior."

Claudia laboriously strapped on her sandal. It was raining and her old bones ached.

"Can the Mother make a mistake?" I finally found the courage to ask.

She looked up. "Why ask me, of all people?"

"Levercham has no business being a Healer. *She* should have been a Herder. Last year she told Boann Bignose she had a tumor when it was obvious to the whole Island that Boann was with child."

"True enough. But Levercham cured the goats of black-leg with only a touch of her hands."

"I thought you didn't believe in the Mother Choice. You've often said it was all so much nonsense."

Claudia sat back in her chair then and put a finger to one of her few remaining teeth and wiggled it. "What I wouldn't give to be able to gnaw on an apple."

I gaped at her. Was she going senile?

"But I can no longer eat unsliced apples or tear meat away from the bone. Nor can I walk up to the orchards without help from two strong lads. What can I still do, old wreck that I am?" She tapped the vellum scroll next to her. "I can read Sextus. And I can stroll the Lady Garden with Nessa."

"I was talking about the Mother Choice!"

"So you were," she said and rose to bid me goodbye.

From the City, Tref Briga is a day and a half ride. The rain continued all the way and I was wet to the hide when Briga, the head-woman, met me at the gate. Her red hair was plastered to her head and there was a smirk on her freckled face. "Sure, I knew there was some great and good reason I didn't drop you into the briny deep when I had the chance." Briga had been on the Gathering that brought me to Avalon. "For here you are again — big, strong, and a Mother-chosen milker. There'll be dancing and feasting amongst the herd tonight."

Mountain humor has always eluded me; Briga knew perfectly well that two-thirds of her herd wouldn't let me near them and the rest bawled like their teats were being torched every time I touched them. I was left with the summer-heifers, who weren't all that delighted, either.

Tref Briga is an old-fashioned Celtic mountain farm — a cluster of round rock-and-thatch houses, byres, and barns, protected by a split-hazel palisade. With its orchards, fields, and meadows, the farm sits on a spur overlooking a placid green valley, across which the Far Hills begin their march to the ocean. When I arrived, the rain had hidden the mountains and turned the village into a quagmire. Looking over Briga's shoulder, I thought I had come to the end of the earth.

In those days, the village was made up of fifteen or so people, four or five of them Briga's womb-children, a large number for an Islander. But Briga loved children and her soul-friend did, too. I never saw Briga's companion there, though; she was one of Arthur's soldiers and on the mainland during that time.

"Dull without her, you know. Might as well be pregnant, so here I am big as a byre already," Briga said as we went into her hall. "And only five months gone. Twins, I expect. I've thrown 'em before, as you know. A gift from the Mother." At our feet, a naked two-year-old was busily trying to tie an old hound bitch's tail to his leg. "Here's one now." She hauled him into her arms and nuzzled his chubby belly. "This is Argante, Kavan. She was here when you were just a wee calf, still wet and wobbly." The child laughed and squirmed in delight. "Where's your sister then, little man?"

"Beer."

"Out in the byre? With Arianrhod and Fuamnach and the cows? Sorcha loves the cows. Gets it from her old man, I expect."

With a kiss on his flat nose, Briga put the baby down next to the hound and showed me my bed along the wall. I muttered a surly thank you and threw myself, still wet, on the bed to have another good cry.

For the next two years, I lived in Briga's hall with her family and an old Herder named Liosliath Longshank, who was so attached to the mountains that she refused to go to the Nursery as a *nainau*. I also spent my bits of spare time with Olwen and Aline, soul-friends who lived in a squat little house next to the palisade. Briga thought them too Romanized, which meant they did not live and breathe cattle, cattle, cattle. I thought them women of some culture and for much the same reason. They owned several books — I'd brought all five of mine — and we often spent summer evenings reading to each other under the apple trees.

Olwen had been called up in the general mobilization before Badon and had fought in that splendid victory. She'd lost half of one of her feet to the battle axe of a young Englishman. But she came home bearing his head. She kept the head, now shrunken and black, on a post outside their door so that everyone who entered could touch it for luck.

But there wasn't much leisure time. Or much luck, either, as far as I was concerned. Mostly, there was work — plowing and planting in the spring; mowing, shearing, gristing in the summer; harvesting and slaughtering in autumn; repairing — house, tool, hedge — in the winter. And always, always, the cows. Never a day without one down with a broken leg, or a breech-born calf, or, at the very least, a sore teat. Still, I did learn to make a good cheese and occasionally even now, Emer, the Hall cheesemaker, will ask me to show her girls how to do my sage cheese.

At the end of planting season, the whole village played hurley in the meadow. Old Longshank minded Briga's new baby while she and the rest of her brood (home from the Child Corps for planting) and I stood Olwen, Aline, and the others. Briga was a ferocious competitor who, for all her good nature, was not above smashing her hurley stick against Olwen's good foot.

"One day, Briga, I'm going to put this foot in your belly and deprive Avalon of half her future population," Olwen called from where she'd fallen.

Briga had by then knocked the horsehide and straw ball into the apple tree goal. "You do and it'll be *your* head on that pole yonder. Say — look! We've got a visitor."

A horse was galloping up the wide grass causeway, its rider clad in the blue tunic of a Hall messenger. Any visitor to Tref Briga was cause for glee, but one from the City demanded a real celebration. The children began to cheer and we all ran toward her. The messenger jumped down from her horse and drew Briga aside. They spoke for a time, during which Briga's hand went suddenly to her mouth.

Turning back to us, Briga said, "Longshank, take the children to the hall. It's cold out here." It was, too. A little snow had fallen a few days before and we had feared for the newly sown crops.

When they had gone, Briga said in a low, flat voice. "The Lady is dead. Murdered at Camelot."

Lile had gone to worship at Ynyswitrin, that hilly island rising out of the marshes of Britain's Summer Region. Later, Nimue, too, often went to its temple, probably as much to be near Camelot and Morgant as to worship. I have never seen it.

From Ynyswitrin Lile went on to Camelot for Beltane. Arthur loved the spring feast and celebrated it in the ancient way, as a Druid festival. Few Druids were left and those few old; nonetheless, Arthur had them performing their nasty rites on his green and driving his cattle through bonfires to protect them from disease. At least that's what the rite's supposed to do, but, frankly, it only succeeds in drying the beasts up for a week. No matter. The Druids weren't what brought people to Camelot at

Beltane. It was the feasting. And the drinking. For the better part of a fortnight, Arthur kept half of Britain falling-down-puking-in-their-boots drunk.

And so they were on the night the Lady of the Lake was butchered in their midst. I had the story from many sources, my own mother among them. Their tales differ in particulars — it happened at that point in a drinking bout when memories flicker — but in the main they agree. The supper, laid out in a typical Pendragon splendor, had been excellent and the singers the finest in the land. The bowls of ale and mead and cider flowed without cease. As a result, the hall was filled with laughter and the joy of springtime.

Arthur, his steel high king's sword beside him, sat with Kai, Gwenhyfar, and Lile at one end of the hall in a small circle, sharing a bowl of Island cider. Behind them stood the men's shieldbearers. Kai's was my old Corpsmate, Balin the Brute, now called Balin the Christian (Kai chose only Christians as his shieldbearers). Arthur's was Medraut, allowed at last into the Pendragon's service.

The little group, like most everyone sober enough to do so, was watching the entertainment — a sword dance performed by four young northerners, nimble boys who seemed to leap about on the very tips of their toes. They tossed and twirled the swords as easily as you and I might a willow cane. Arthur cheered as the swords flew higher and in ever-widening circles. Even Kai appeared amused.

My mother and Lile were less interested. They were discussing the difficulties of a voyage from

Avalon so early in the year. I suspect it was Gwenhyfar doing most of the discussing. She certainly would have had no trouble making herself heard; that shrill voice could penetrate to the rafters of any banqueting hall.

"My *dear* Lady," she said, with a sweep of her arm that barely cleared Lile's long nose. "Last time I journeyed to Avalon, it was the *worst*, positively the *worst* voyage I'd ever been on. Save *perhaps* one to the *Orkneys*. And you *know* what *that* is. I spent the entire time retching, actually *heaving*, over the side." She reached out to touch Lile.

Gwenhyfar's hand fell on a headless shoulder.

A single sword stroke had decapitated Lile. Her body twitched twice before it collapsed, a bloody fountain. Her head rolled across the pine floor and came to rest against Arthur's right foot. He stared down at it a moment, then, with a little moan, vomited into Gwenhyfar's lap.

With a shout, Kai leaped up and immediately half a dozen warriors wrestled the sword dancers to the floor. They died there. And when Arthur at last recovered himself, he calmed the hall by exclaiming that justice had been done.

The problem was, at that moment, a horse was pounding down Camelot's causeway, carrying Lile's killer into the safety of the night. Only when someone finally thought to examine the dancers' swords did Arthur find he'd executed four innocent lads. Their swords were clean.

He ordered the hall doors locked then and sent for the keeper of the main gate. Arthur and Kai, joined now by Lancelot and Morgant, received him in the King's rooms. Bedwyr had been left to deal with the mess in the hall.

The gatekeeper told them about the hooded rider and his fast horse.

"Did you recognize him?" Kai asked, settling his bulk into Arthur's chair.

"Not him. His horse," the gatekeeper said. "He was an old man, veteran of many battles, and wore his grey hair swept back from his face and dressed with lard, in the old Celtic manner.

"How very observant." Kai laced his fingers together and rested them on his belly, thumbs tapping. "And what horse was that?"

"His name's Blueshot. A big grey. Fast, too. From the Lady Line, he is," the old man answered. No one had yet bothered to tell him what had happened.

A purple flush began at Kai's pale neck, then splotched over his face. "*Whose* horse?" he asked in a soft whisper.

"Why, Balin's. Balin the Christian's," the old warrior said in a perplexed voice. "Blueshot won't let anyone else on him. He —"

Just then, Bedwyr burst into the room, stinking of sweat and fear (so Lancelot told me). "The King's sword —" He had trouble getting the words out. "It's . . . it's gone!" Bedwyr fell to his knees. "The Lady's head, too."

Arthur himself accompanied Lile's body back to Avalon. Throughout the week of her funeral games, he looked tired and bewildered, but we assumed that when he returned to Logres, he would act to have Balin brought in and executed. But at mid-summer and Nimue's Lady-making, Balin was still free. Nor

112

was he in Arthur's hands by autumn. It was then that Nimue decided Avalon would have to avenge its own — a decision she should have made three breaths after the Mother chose her Lady.

Balin, she knew, had headed north, probably for his father's *dun* in Reged. But there had been no word that he'd actually arrived there. He might still be hiding in one of Britain's thick forests. Therefore, it would be unwise, Nimue told the Nine, to risk a century of Daughters in an attack against Dun Urien's heavily defended rings. "If the Brute goes to ground, *then* we can smoke him out. First, we need to find him." To do so, she would send a half-section of hand-picked young scouts: Faencha, whose skill with swords was not limited to their making; Branwen, late Chief Centurion of the Child Corps, so much the natural leader that the whole Island took it for granted she would be Lady when the time came; and Rhiannon, called the Hound, because she was so good a tracker.

The surprise was that I was included, thanks to some hard argument by Nimue. She told the Nine (so she said later) that not only was I a crack shot with the sling, I also had a genius for disguise. "Genius" was *her* word; I can hardly see how a few hours pretending to be an English goddess could be construed as evidence of genius. Although I must admit that even now I can imitate almost any female voice I want to — and a good many male ones, too, come to that. And, it's true, I am a pretty fair actor. Matter of fact, I suspect there are several people on Avalon who think I've been playing Lady of the Lake for some years now.

On the surface, our little troop seemed a most

peculiar miscellany. But Nimue wasn't *that* foolish. She had chosen the four of us because we got along well and our talents blended. Besides, Branwen, a superb leader, could issue a command without being degrading or arrogant and was good-natured enough to be willing to do her share of the dirty work. As a result, she got the best out of her soldiers. Even me. Even the Hound.

The Hound. In all the years we've been friends — and we truly are friends, though we often have cause not to be — I can never remember the Hound speaking good of anyone. Or speaking at all, really. She always seems to snarl. A real cur of a woman, except — except she's so beautiful, with her black hair and eyes lighter than her face. The combination of her beauty and her churlishness is devastating.

Now she is Chief Gatherer, the youngest in memory, and does the job so well that Avalon's population would no doubt have doubled, were it not for this drought. I worry about her, though, because in the process, she's pushed herself so hard that last winter she developed a dry cough she can't seem to shake. Nor will she take time to see the Healers, not even when her flesh is withering like Avalon's wheat.

But on that September day when we were eighteen, the four of us stood before Nimue strong and handsome as young horses. And, I suspect, as mindless. As Lady, I would never have sent unseasoned girls on such a mission. I would have recalled two or three reliable old sweats. But I have long since realized that I have neither the imagination nor the faith Nimue had. She always acted out of love, whereas I have chosen the easier

114

course and act out of what I like to think of as common sense. I have long since realized, too, that Nimue had the better part.

She bade us on our way with the full ritual of Adventuring. She knelt on the shale of the beach, the Nine standing behind her and the Sacred Bull beside her.

Meara, Lile's soul-friend was there, too, by herself a little ways away, her face grey and closed. Meara was already growing strange and solitary. Not long afterward she went to live alone as a charcoal burner in the Forest of Light with a few cats for company. I can only remember seeing her twice after that. Once at my Lady-making and again when this terrible drought left that end of the Island in flames and she came to pray at the Crystal Shrine. Before anyone could stop her, she sacrificed a striped cat that she'd brought with her in a basket.

Nimue raised her knuckle to her lips in salute to our courage. Then she stood and handed us our two blue leather pouches, one filled with protective herbs, the other with Avalon's sweet earth. I took the dirt without comment.

"The Mother is; the Daughters go forth," Nimue began the litany.

"Now and always," we answered. In those days, there was no irony in that response. But that was before Arthur's arrogance again set war loose in Britain. In those days, the Lady could send young women to the mainlands in the knowledge that at least some of them could come back.

I have very little recollection of the voyage to Lyonesse. I suspect we sang. I do remember the weather was good, the sea calm. On debarking, our orders were to go directly to Calchvynydd, the small realm now ruled by our Child Corps comrade, Elin. There, we were to rest and give ear to any rumors that might have trickled in about Balin's whereabouts. We were not — "I repeat, NOT to go to Camelot. Argante, you understand me, I'm sure." I did.

The trip to Calchvynydd was as uneventful as the voyage had been. The Lady Lyonesse, secretly informed of our mission, provided us with good horses and ample, if rather plain, provisions. And, for once, the late summer weather on the British mainland was splendid. Only once did we have to plug through a day-long drizzle. We sang all the way.

On the sixth day, we entered the forest that ringed Elin's palace. It was a dark, silent place. A thick carpet of moss and wet leaves muffled the sound of horses' hooves. Great oaks crowded the winding path so closely the horses often stumbled over roots. From time to time, we had to dismount to avoid low branches.

"Let's sing some more," I suggested, uneasy in the forest's brooding presence.

"Oh, Argante. I've sung so much now I feel like I'm swallowing sand," Faencha replied.

"Argante's scared. Probably thinks the Grey Ones are about to get her." This from the Hound, ever compassionate.

"Well, I'm kind of scared, too," said Branwen, glancing at the impenetrable green wall that surrounded us. "This woods —" She didn't finish. Instead, she launched into a very spirited, very bawdy Corps campsong, which Faencha and I took up immediately.

Singing at the top of our lungs, we picked our way slowly along, the Hound in the lead, followed by Branwen, Faencha, then me, nervously bringing up the rear.

We had just ended the song when a sound like the creak of a wooden floor made me look up. As I did, someone — or something — dropped out of a tree and wrenched me from the saddle. I fell hard and heard my ankle crunch under our combined weights.

"Grey Ones!" I screamed. Even as I did, my companions reacted in the perfect harmony of battle that the Daughters are drilled in almost from the cradle. As her horse wheeled, Branwen's spear was already in her hand, her body coiled to hurl it at the enemy. In one motion, Faencha leaped from her horse and charged, shield up close to her chin, sword at the ready. The Hound jumped back to protect the weakest flank.

Branwen had quick reflexes and a sharp eye. She could judge a situation and act on it in the same instant. She flung her spear with no concern that it might hit me as I struggled with the attacker. Indeed, there was no need for concern. Branwen could pierce a three-inch ring from fifty yards away at a full gallop. In battle, she literally did not know fear or confusion. As warrior, as woman, she put herself completely in the hands of the Mother.

The spear struck the attacker in the side and he — it — rolled off me, screaming and clawing at the wound, from which thick dark blood spurted.

Faencha, on top of the hooded figure now, gave it a hard kick in the head and it lay still. She yanked the spear out of the thing's side, then flipped it onto its stomach, the point of her sword pressed to the back of its neck.

"Well, it's no Grey One," Branwen said as she looked down at the bleeding attacker. "Nor English, by the clothes. Must be a bandit." She dismounted and came to take a look at me where I sat giggling from fright and shock. "Can you stand?"

"My dear Centurion, not only can I stand, I believe I can at last fly. Here, I'll demonstrate —"

Before I could try either, Branwen pushed me flat on my back, stuck her shield under the ankle, then looked around for a couple of stout sticks to use as a splint. Meanwhile, our captive began to moan and twist. Faencha's only response was to dig her sword point in deeper. The Hound, just then riding past to check the track behind us, glanced down. She pulled her horse up sharp and sat looking at the prisoner with her head cocked to the side as dogs do when they're a bit puzzled. Abruptly, she dismounted and pulled the hood back.

It was Elin.

While I giggled and Branwen and Faencha gaped, the Hound jerked off her neck-scarf to stanch the flow of blood from Elin's wound. Branwen found voice first. "The fool. Of course, she knew we were on our way and thought she'd give us a surprise welcome. I should have expected it. She was always arrogant. Now, I suppose we've managed to kill the Queen of Calchvynydd."

For the moment my ankle was forgotten as the three of them worked over Elin. It was a very bad few moments and I did nothing to help matters by chortling away and offering bits of advice like, "Hang her by her toes. That way the blood'll run to her head and not out her side." Elin must have been conscious when I said that because forever after, anytime I acted unreasonably she would suggest I be hanged upside down so that my silly ideas would run to my head and not out my mouth.

My memory of the rest of the incident is very dim and only becomes clear several days later. I do recall being hauled through the forest on a litter, in terrible pain.

My ankle was badly broken and it was obvious I wouldn't be able to pursue Balin with the rest. "We'll have to go without you," Faencha informed me. She spoke softly and there was pity in her brown eyes. "We've heard the Brute's on the move again. Still heading north. We have to leave immediately if we're going to catch him before he gets to his father's lands."

I cursed. In three languages and two dialects. Faencha was sensible enough not to try to mollify me, but let my anger and disappointment run their course. Finally, she took my hand and said, "I believe this whole adventure is part of our destiny. And your broken ankle, too. We cannot change it."

Of course, she was right. No one can alter destiny by rage or tears or broken bones. But it took me another five years and the loss of almost everyone I ever loved to understand as much. I certainly did not understand when the next day at dawn I lay on a linen-covered cot and watched the three of them ride into the morning mist.

Chapter Eight

The coughing-sickness almost took Deirdre. I'm glad it didn't. I'd have missed her pompous bossiness. Which, I might say, has not been lessened by her proximity to death. If anything, it's gotten worse. She seems to believe she's Goddess-touched because, somehow, she avoided meeting Arawn, the Lord of the Other World. As if she, and not the Healers, prevented it.

The young guards, Flann and Macha, helped me escape Deirdre yesterday. They reminded me it was Oimelc, the Mother's own festival. It's never celebrated with the merry commotion of the other seasonal feasts; winter, though dying, often rallies for a final round of dirty weather. But it was time for me to drink the Mother-drop, the last cupful of juice from the previous apple harvest, preserved until now. Afterward, we sat in the garden under an unusually warm winter sun and drank real cider, sweet, aged, fermented. They asked me to tell them what I'd been writing. Cheeky, of course, but flattering. I told them a bit about Nimue sending the four of us after Balin, and Elin's foolish trick and how she hadn't died of it.

Like me, she needed to convalesce, though did so much more slowly; her wound was very serious indeed. When I could hobble around a bit, I began to visit her in her dog- and book-littered room. For over a week, she didn't know who I was. And when she was finally able to sort me out from the myriad aunts, sisters, and maid-servants who hovered around her, she hardly acknowledged me. Perhaps her embarrassment at having been felled by four Gatherlings was too great to permit more than a surly hello-I'm-better-today-thank-you.

Even though she was by then out of danger, she still slept most of the time and I often sat by her bed with one or the other of her aunts. They clearly adored her and, as loving kinswomen will, talked incessantly about her. I learned her favorite food was pigeon pie; that as an infant she talked early and walked late; that she was affectionate and easy-going with her little sisters.

I heard again the story of how she decided her hands could heal, of the drowned boy and the breath she beat back into him. This time, though, I also heard that the next year she cried for two days when her hound pup caught a chill and she could not save it. "She's been trying to make up for it ever since," Elin's aunt said, sweeping her arm around the room. "Look at these smelly hounds."

Eventually, she was sent to the Island, to learn the healing arts. And, as she once told me, "I also learned I can't cure everything. A bit of wisdom *you* should experiment with, Argante."

She had left Avalon when she was not quite seventeen and spent almost a year on campaign with Arthur's army, acquitting herself, her aunts assured me, with honor and courage. Then, a little more than a year before, her father and mother died suddenly of a fever and Elin, the first-born of a sonless family, had come home as Queen.

Her initial problem, not yet completely solved when I came to Calchvynydd, was to convince her nobles that, though young and female, she could protect the country from the English. They had not known woman rule in a generation or two and in the first few months after her father's death, five or six had packed up their gold and families and fled across the channel to Armorica, leaving their estates to be tended by overseers. But since then, what looked to be a flood of emigration had slowed to a thin trickle as Elin demonstrated her ability to command and negotiate.

I think she must have been weighted down terribly by the task of keeping her domain intact. She was, after all, just turned twenty, still in many ways the girl she'd been on Avalon, queen and physician notwithstanding. And so, to get away from the greybeards that surrounded her, she had decided to play brigand and drop out of an oak tree onto four unsuspecting old friends.

As she continued to grow stronger, the greybeards came back, displacing the kinswomen at her bedside, and, once again, she was hard at the task of administering her realm. Even so, in the evenings she would call us into her apartment to listen to her middle sister sing and to her eldest aunt's tales of her time as a hostage in Ireland. That good woman always ended by proudly reminding us that her father had bought her back for five times her honor-price. Sometimes, too, I would read to the little assemblage.

Surprisingly, considering her apparent distaste for me on Avalon, Elin liked to hear me read and so I began to visit her rooms in the mornings for breakfast. "Nothing like a little Galenus when you've got porridge in your mouth," she'd say. "But you've got a good accent. Claudia may be an ignorant old imposter as far as philosophy goes, but at least she teaches real Latin and not that soft goo the Christians get from their priests."

Breakfast was a great ritual with Elin. Even on campaign or with a surgery full of patients, she took every care that it be delicious and festive. I have forgotten what we ate in that sunlit room: porridge, of course, and eggs, surely, served in terra cotta and silver. What I do remember is Elin.

She wasn't spectacularly beautiful like the Hound or striking like Faencha, but tall and handsome — and smart enough to make the best of her looks. There in her villa, she wore a plain linen stola, pink or pale yellow to show off her dusky skin, but with no jewelry, not even a torque. When I arrived in the mornings, her dark hair would already be dressed for the day, knotted in the severe Roman manner and also without ornament. She used cosmetics, though, which no native Islander did, kohl around her deep brown eyes and a sweet musk. I smell it sometimes in my dreams and wake in tears.

Elin would not approve. She disliked displays of emotion, just as she disliked idle conversation. I, of course, bawl easily and quack constantly, a burden she bore with the same degree of patience she permitted the whinier of her hounds. She herself shed few tears and only spoke when her words had been sorted and weighed. Not that she was cold. Hardly that. It was, I think, that except in the matter of dogs, she didn't limit her elegance to her clothes. At the time this difference between us worried me. Now, I realize it was part of our attraction for each other.

Don't think me completely naive. I was quite aware that I desired her. Had even on Avalon. And how not? On Avalon, sex was no mystery. Corpsmates knew each others' bodies as soon as there was hair between their legs. I had spent many a night in Faencha's bed. Niall's, too, for that matter. Branwen had often brought me glowing pleasure and I her. It meant nothing, was nothing but the groping of half-grown children. Here, though, in Elin's stylish villa, I somehow felt reluctant to suggest a spot of country pleasure.

It wasn't because of the enmity we felt for each other as children — my bruised ribs, her broken nose; all that had been laughed out of existence long before. Perhaps, I conjectured, it was because we really were slenderly acquainted. Oh, we'd endured

Claudia together, eaten at the same table, sometimes shared the same drinking horn. But after Cadwallon told us about Annis and Arthur, I avoided Elin as much as possible. Perhaps my guilt lay between us — guilt about not believing a dead boy; guilt about my father playing accomplice to Annis. Anyway, Elin terrified me and not just because of her self-contained manner or her sudden violence.

Now, though, I was no longer afraid. Nevertheless, our conversation seemed limited to discussions of the more ponderous Latin philosophers. Perhaps the barrier was her life here in her villa, so alien to me. And not particularly pleasing.

For instance: when we sat down to breakfast (when *I* sat; Elin reclined in the languid and, to my mind, distressingly erotic Roman way), we were served by an aging English slave. Sometimes, when he brought out a new dish, a ragout or a savory we didn't recognize, Elin would tease him, saying, "This is it, Argante. Wilbert has finally found a way to get free. Poison. A bite or two, some moans, four heels drumming on the floor, and he'll be back in Middel Seaxe before nightfall."

The old slave, skinny and sharp-beaked as a shorebird, continued to ladle from the tureen. "Couldn't I just. But not before I'd set the place on fire and dug up that gold you've got hid in the well."

"And violated all us womenfolk, too, I suppose."

The old man delicately spooned up a mushroom. "Especially that."

This kind of talk made me nervous. It had always seemed to me that a slave, if he had any sense at all, would seize the first opportunity to escape his servitude — and wreak whatever chaos he could in the process. When Wilbert had gone, I said, "Aren't you putting ideas in his head? Even if he's old."

Elin smiled gently, as she did at not very bright hound pups. "I know you'll find this hard to believe, Daughter of Avalon, but three generations of Calchvynydd sovereigns have offered Wilbert his freedom. He won't take it."

"By the Mother, why not?" I was incredulous.

"Says he loves us." When Elin reached for her ale cup, the movement must have disturbed her wound. A pair of sharp lines appeared between her eyebrows and the color drained from her face. "Not much of an excuse, eh?" she muttered between clenched teeth.

"Certainly not," I said as helplessly I watched her pain reach its crest.

I made no further mention of the slaves. But mainland life, I found, left me a bit queasy.

The library, of course, was something else again. I never dreamed so many books existed. There must have been forty or fifty of them rolled up in the cedar pigeon holes that lined one whole wall. By the time Elin was up and around, I'd worked my way through Tacitus, Lucian, and Seneca. I'd dipped into Apuleius, too, but somehow I didn't find his donkey nearly so funny as Tacitus's Celts. Wherever had that man picked up such bizarre fictions?

One afternoon, as I lay on the marble floor reading, Elin came in unexpectedly. I had thought she was busy with the greybeards, but, she explained, she'd grown tired of them. "Why are you on the cold floor, Argante? There are couches aplenty in here and —" She grinned. "If they're too soft for your Island butt, a desk chair."

I scowled. She'd put her finger on the reason why I'd chosen the floor and I found myself feeling like a savage. Damn your Romanized elegance, I wanted to say. I'd like to yank the silver pins out of your fine linen dress and wallow naked on the marble with you until we wore out both our butts.

Of course, I didn't say that. In fact, I said nothing at all. After a moment or two, she left.

Soon Elin decided she was well enough to take outdoor exercise (this against the advice of her physicians, whom she promptly sent packing) and show me around her estate. "You need some exercise, too. That leg'll go stiff on you. Those fools are criminal to have kept you in so long." I let the doctors catch the blame though I could have spent the rest of my life inside Elin's house.

Dun Calchvynydd was not an ancient fortress clutching the edge of a cliff or squatting atop a hill hidden behind half a dozen rock rings. It was a fine villa, thoroughly fortified, yes, but also, as I've said, thoroughly civilized. Elin took great pride in its handsomely mosaicked rooms and checkered marble hallways.

The courtyard, with its benches and herb garden, was her special favorite. Its walls and floor were decorated with portrayals of Celtic and Roman deities — Lug and Dagda, Mars and Mercury, even a depiction of a scarlet-robed Lady of the Lake with the green hills of Avalon spreading away behind her.

Just off the courtyard stood a little shrine to the Mother. In it we often knelt together, once sacrificing a pigeon in thanksgiving for our restored health. Later, Elin's soothsayer poked at its entrails and announced that our lives would be long and full. If that was all having the coveted "Sight" amounted to, I decided, then mainlanders were even simpler than I thought.

In the shrine's outer wall, there was an alcove that held some strange objects. On closer inspection they appeared to be bits of dried-out incense and soap and, I think, fennel. I looked at them often, trying to puzzle out their meaning, until one day Elin said, "Those are propitiations to the English goddess Freyr."

I turned around, confused. She leaned back against the shrine's low porch rail and crossed her arms. "I'm English, you know."

My jaw dropped to my penannular and she laughed out loud. "My mother was, anyway," she said.

It seems that, after a long war, Elin's grandfather had finally won an uneasy peace with his English neighbors. But there continued to be nasty incidents — isolated farms burned and pillaged, cattle mutilated, slaves kidnapped. When his nobles began to rattle their spears and cry out for another war, the old king decided to try a different tack. He offered to marry his eldest son to the English king's daughter. "The Englishman took the offer gladly," Elin said as I joined her against the porch rail.

"He knew they would've gotten the worst of it in another war because by then my grandfather had allied himself with the Pendragon. So it was convenient all the way around — the kingdoms got peace, the nobles got to fight in Arthur's wars, and I

129

got born." She touched her hair, her dark, dark hair shot through with streaks the red of a winter sunset.

"Not that it was that simple," she said.

"Your poor mother must have been pretty lonesome. And scared, too, plunked down all alone in a strange place with a strange man," I said, wanting to make up for my previous lack of grace, wanting, most of all, to please Elin.

"Alone! Hardly." She laughed again. "Stanhild brought a retinue of twenty-five people, bond and free, and cattle enough to fill ten byres. To say nothing of the dozen mules that carried her trunks."

Stanhild's riches helped, of course, and she was a king's daughter, a future king's wife. Still, it was a position I wouldn't have liked to find myself in. A few hours among hostile strangers had taught me that. But Stanhild had fared well. She turned out to have a Celt's heart in her English bosom. She was a naturally warm, happy person, and full of fun. She was also smart. Within the first month, she had visited every clansman's house. By the second month, she'd been to see every peasant and slave. All had received gifts according to their stations and each the dazzling Stanhild smile.

"Half the men in Calchvynydd were in love with her, I think," Elin said. "And my father never took a second wife. Even when he became king, him with nothing but daughters. Oh, she had charm on her all right."

I rocked back and forth on the railing, wanting to say how like her mother she must be. "And a child soon shows from what root she's risen, eh?"

was all I could manage. Though I meant it to be light and complimentary, it came out sounding flat.

Elin looked confused, then embarrassed. "I'm sorry, Argante. I didn't mean to carry on about my family like that when you don't know — I mean when you haven't got . . . I mean . . ."

She touched my face.

I fell over the porch rail.

Fortunately, I landed on my shoulder, not my injured leg, and only sprained the shoulder. Elin's excellent care and a good night's sleep fixed me up quickly enough. The next morning, when she came to check on me, I was already dressed. It had been a struggle, with my arm feeling the way it did, but I'd managed to get on my tunic and a pair of sandals.

Elin wore her usual stola, this one a soft buff color. For a change her hair wasn't done in a knot. It fell in thick waves around her shoulders. "Good to see you up and around," she said. "I was worried about you last night. I came in about midnight and you were moaning and tossing in your sleep."

"I was?"

"I stayed a while. Until you settled down."

"Oh. Thanks." I couldn't think of anything else to say.

"Let's see the arm."

I sat on the couch and began fumbling at my tunic.

"Here, let me do that," she said. As she carefully pulled off the tunic, her hand brushed my breast. I wanted her to touch it, stroke it, take it in her mouth.

When I saw my nipples grown hard, I felt myself blush.

"Don't be embarrassed," she said with a little smile. "It's a natural reaction. To the cold air."

I tried to laugh but my throat was dry as parched moorland.

She bent over me to examine my shoulder, squeezing it here and there, asking me to move it this way and that. She was so close I could smell her herb-scented hair.

When she finished, I thought she'd move away. But her hands hovered above my shoulders — like birds whose flight has been stopped by a sudden wind.

Then her hands were in my hair, her lips on my throat, on my eyes, my mouth. With a flash of desire like lightning, I was swept into the hot storm of her love.

Its thunder roared in my ears as she drew her tongue along my lips and moved her fingers lightly down my back. I pulled the pearl-tipped pins out of her stola and stepped back as she shrugged it off to stand naked before me. Her body was the color of fresh cream. Almost without volition, I dropped to my knees and buried my face in her belly to taste its sweet warmth. My womb leapt as she put her hands in my hair, then slid them down to cup my breasts. I moved toward the dark hair of her mons.

"Wait," she said, gently raising me to my feet, caressing my throat with her mouth as I slipped out of my trousers. "You first."

Pushing me onto the bed, she covered me with

her scented body and sucked my tongue into her mouth. Slowly, rhythmically, she began to thrust against me until my loin throbbed hot and wet. My hands found her breasts as I ground my body up into hers.

She pulled away then and turned me over. I felt the heat of her breath as her tongue slid slowly down my spine making wet little spirals that sent my senses spinning.

Finally, I could wait no longer. "Now," I whispered, hoarse and trembling with desire. With a moan, I turned to her ravening mouth. It glided over me, tongue licking at my breasts, my belly, until at last she found the hard, hot kernel of my craving. I lunged against her again and again as she brought me to shattering ecstasy.

The autumn passed. Outside the villa, the oaks turned bronze and gold and rust, then lost their leaves so that they seemed to form a great grey cocoon around our world, sealing me away from thoughts of Balin or Lile. Sometimes, though, we emerged from Elin's bed to take excursions into the walled farmyard, both of us limping heavily through its mud.

Cold, bare, wet though it is, late autumn has its charms, nowhere more so than in the bustle of a large farm preparing for winter. From the smokehouses, fires of oak bark and old reeds sent their sweet smoke cascading around barn and villa. Black-handed young bondsmen scrubbed the hypocausts while others, their hands covered with blood, worked the slaughter-floor. Women stood sweating over lard-rendering vats, dogs a few steps behind, on their stomachs, ears up, eyes wide. The dull ring of the blacksmith's hammer blended with the lowing of the doves in their cotes and the laughter of the milkmaids.

Soon, Elin decided she'd been housebound too long and announced that the slaughter would henceforth be done under her direction — much to the old bailiff's annoyance. And much to mine because she insisted I help. Now, I've always been bored numb by the process of choosing which cow or pig will be served up on the winter table and which will still be snuffling straw come spring. Furthermore, I'd not yet slaked my lust for her.

I refused. We quarreled.

The details need not concern us now, except to say it was loud, nasty, and public.

Finally, unable to win and more than unwilling to lose, I stalked off (as well as I could, leaning heavily on a stick) across the harvested grain fields; slowly at first, in part because the stiff remains of wheat slowed me down but also because I expected Elin to follow me. When I realized she wasn't going to, I speeded up a bit, until the villa and its outbuildings were out of sight and I found myself on the edge of the oak forest.

I sat down on an old stump to rest — and nourish my anger and self-righteousness. Elin had, I told myself, no right to think that just because she suddenly wanted to play chatelaine, I should be expected to help. She knew perfectly well I loathed cattle, dead or alive. She was, I decided, trying to humiliate me.

"How like her. Nothing exists but what *she*

wants," I said out loud. "Well, I just hope some cow gores her good and she has *two* holes in her belly."

"Ain't a very nice thing to wish on anybody," a voice said behind me.

I leaped up and whirled around, then sat abruptly back down — my ankle wouldn't hold. A ginger-haired woman-soldier stood before me, grinning.

"You Argante of Avalon?" she asked. "I bet you are. They told me to look for a tall skinny girl with a bad foot and worse temper."

"I am Argante," I said with what I thought was the greatest of dignity.

"Och, you are. They also said you was a pompous young chit."

"Why do you seek me?"

At that, she began to laugh. She laughed so hard she actually doubled over, then hopped around on one leg. I gave her the cold, hard look I had carefully developed when I was in the upper ranks of the Child Corps. Though it was guaranteed to quell a pack of ten-year-olds, the only effect it had on this evil-smelling old trooper was to set her laughing the harder.

I got up to leave.

"Wait, young madam. I got a letter from the Island, from the Lady." She held out a leather packet bearing the ocean-blue seal of the ruler of Avalon.

I had never seen the woman before and she wore the uniform of Arthur's cavalry. So, before I took the letter, I asked, as noncommittally as possible, "How did you come by this?"

"It's high time you should be asking. For all you

know, I'm one of Arthur's hired assassins, come to do the job Kai didn't get done before Gwenhyfar packed you off to the Island."

"I think if you were, I would never have gotten up off this stump. Besides, I'm not worried about Arthur's having me killed at this late date. For one thing, he knows I serve the Mother. For another, he no longer cares whether I exist or not. Now, madam, you haven't answered my question. Who are you and where did you get that letter?"

"Here, take it. It'll explain everything." She stuck the packet in my hand. "And while you read, I'm after catching a little nap." She spread her cloak over the damp ground and was snoring before I got the seal broken.

The letter was indeed from Nimue, written in the code she'd explained before we left Avalon. I shifted around on the stump till I was comfortable, then translated it slowly:

"Argante: The woman bearing this message is Meredydd of Lystynes. She has served the Lady of the Lake for many years, sometimes at the risk of her own life. She will accompany you on the journey I'm now asking you to take. Meredydd plays at being a rough soldier, but she is a king's heir. Rely on her and heed her advice.

"We have had definite word as to Balin's movements and his present whereabouts. The situation is even more serious than I first believed. Annis is involved. It appears she long ago suborned Balin by convincing him that the fall of Avalon, preceded by the death of the Lady, would establish Christianity as the religion of the Celtic Realms. I'm told she made him believe she was the mother of the Christian god. And then seduced him. Apparently there's no end to the woman's tricks nor to Christian gullibility.

"Once he had killed Lile, he was to hand over her head to Annis's agents. Then, having gotten rid of the evidence, he could proceed to her fortress in the Wastelands in his own time, enjoying the protection of his sundry kinsmen along the way."

I turned the page. How did Balin come by Lile's head? It had disappeared, with the steel high king's sword, *after* he had fled Camelot. The question didn't appear to concern Nimue; her letter continued:

"It was a good plan — Annis would have Lile's head and quickly, and we would be chasing Balin through half the kingdoms of Britain. But I've come up with a plan of my own. Before the snow flies, you and the bearer of this letter are to go to Lystynes, King Pellam's land. Pellam is my messenger's brother and has agreed to help us in this matter."

She continued with an outline of her plan to foil Annis. It involved Scathach, the fierce Highland queen to whom Avalon's Warriors were sent to learn winter warfare. Branwen, Faencha, and the Hound were already with her.

I read quickly through the rest, hoping I would not be included in any more of the plan. I was. The letter ended: "The Mother is; the Daughters go forth."

And that was an order. If it had come a month earlier, I would have leaped to obey. But by now all I wanted to do was spend the rest of my life with Elin, up to my waist in books and dogs. Slaves, too, if that's what she wanted.

I sat on the stump staring at the letter, then at Meredydd. I thought seriously of killing her in mid snore. Instead, I just cried.

Chapter Nine

After awhile, Meredydd woke and we walked
back to the villa. Elin was sitting in the courtyard, a
book in front of her, the stink of the barnyard now
scrubbed away and replaced by a heavy Italian
musk. I had never known anyone who smelled so
good. She rose when she saw us, eyebrows twitching
as they did when she was pleased. She was prepared
to forgive and by then I had forgotten we'd ever
been feuding, so disturbed was I at the prospect of
having to leave Calchvynydd. She came forward to

embrace me, but I stood stiff in her arms and she backed away.

"All right, Argante, if you want to go on being mad, that's entirely up to you." She turned toward her guest. I burst into tears.

Meredydd, who had been watching this little scene, came to my rescue. "I know you, Healer. You saved me an eye two springs ago up in the Brecons. Now it looks like *you're* the one nearly blind. You best take another peek at this girl."

I still couldn't talk, but through my tears I tried to give her a grateful look. Elin turned back to me, touching my arm lightly in confusion. "What is it? What's the matter?"

My only response was to blubber even louder.

Elin stared at me in consternation until finally Meredydd said, "I've come with a message from the Island ordering this Daughter to get on with the pursuit of Balin the Brute. It looks like she don't want to."

"But I must."

Elin scowled and pulled at her lower lip. "But not right away, surely. Winter's coming on. You wouldn't get very far. It could wait till spring, couldn't it?" She turned to Meredydd.

"The Lady seems pretty sure Argante ought to go right now. So's she can get to Lystynes before hard winter sets in."

Elin continued to pull her lip and I continued to weep. Then she gave a sharp nod. "I'll go, too," she announced and immediately began to shout for her servants to start packing.

Meredydd caught her arm and said, "Lady Elin, I

140

know you for a good doctor and a brave one. I seen you pull lads right out from under King Hadugat's spears, then send 'em home to their mams fit as the day they left. And I can see there's . . . um . . . something between you and this girl. But, truth to tell, you ain't been invited on this little trip. And even if you was, by the look of you I don't think you'd get very far."

"Of course Elin can come along! She's a good soldier. You said so yourself. And her wound's lots better." I had found my voice at last and Elin's decision to join us made me brave enough to defy not just Meredydd but the Lady herself, if necessary.

"She's right, you know," Elin said in her most imperious tone. "I'm quite good as new."

Elin and I now stood shoulder to shoulder staring at Meredydd, arms crossed and legs planted firmly in the wide stance that as children we learned was the carriage of command. Once again, we were comrades of the Child Corps, united before the enemy. Meredydd, bless her heart, did us the courtesy of not laughing, though she must have been amused by these two posturing puppies.

Her silence led me to believe she was beginning to waver and I wanted to finish strong. Meredydd was not a very young woman, so with the ignorant brutality of youth, I said, "The country between here and Lystynes might be pretty rough for you," I said. "A physician would be —"

Elin grabbed my arm. "What Argante means—"

Meredydd cut her off with a laugh. "My Lady Elin, I don't care if you come along or not. But if you do, you better bring some bandages to stop up this girl's mouth. Now, I'd like me a bath, something to eat, and a spot to sleep in. We'll start in the morning."

Elin blushed deep into her dark hairline and hugged me to her. My face in the wool of her cloak, I trembled with our victory.

That night Meredydd and Elin ate in the hall with her clan's warband — I had no desire to hear the howls of that wolf-pack when she told them she planned to go adventuring without them. Afterward, the two joined me in the library, where Meredydd, the stench of Arthur's cavalry more or less washed away by a very brief bath and several bottles of Rhenish wine, commenced to tell us how things stood in Camelot.

"I tell you, the King ain't the man he was. Too much of the drink. Leaves too much to Kai these days. Well, maybe not when he's sober. He's still a good enough man then. Still a great man then, I suppose. But nobody knows how soon he'll be drunk again and what he'll do. Or, worse yet, *let* be done, once he puts a paw around a drinking horn. Been that way ever since he started trying to take on foreign nations. Morgant the Merlin Falcon told him to stick to the English and let the Cornish and the Welsh protect their own coasts. But, no, he would carry his army to Gaul. And take a licking. Now it's Ireland." Meredydd waved her empty cup and Elin filled it with still more of the Rhenish wine.

"Anyhow, about Balin," Meredydd continued. "After Arthur let Balin and the Lady's head *and* the sword get away — and *after* he sobered off, Arthur was scared, let me tell you. And he should've been. Think about it. The Lady of the Lake — who done more for him than six armies could have — murdered in his own hall. By one of his own men. Oh, it's scared he was.

"So he calls on Cormac mac Cormac, a young Scot who just come down to join us. A great black beast of a boy and good with sword or spear. A fighting man out of a centurion's dream. But with a manner soft as an Irishwoman's ass. Arthur sends this lad after Balin with only a couple of bondsmen for company. Well, it was plain too late. By then Balin had got to safety and poor Cormac went walking into half a century of Annis's Grey Ones. They sent him back to Camelot in little pieces. Arthur wailed for two days and the dogs with him. But he didn't send nobody else. Still ain't. Says his other men are too busy fighting the King of Leinster right now. Says he'll wait till spring."

Meredydd slurped the wine and shook her head. "I tell you, Arthur ain't the man he was. And lots of folks're starting to see it. Morgant, especially. She near went crazy when he said he couldn't spare nobody else to hunt Balin down. I was in the guard room when she come out of Arthur's apartment that night. Had her cloak up over her head and was heaving curses in the old language like a Christian smashing up a Roman temple. 'No good will come of this. . .' she yells, skinny little arm pointed straight at the King's heart. 'I fear for you and for the Realms, oh man of dust! Seven kingdoms will be reduced to poverty and desolation by your folly!' And then she swept out of there all swirling cloak and dark looks. Us soldiers in the guard room was scared, I can tell you. But all Arthur done was call for more ale."

She shook her head again. "Now, it's bad enough the King's got no intention of avenging Lile or even Cormac, but he's let the Sword fall into Annis's hands. Seems like all him and Kai can think about now is fighting the King of Leinster. It was Morgant sent word to the Island about it all. Her and Nimue was lovers a long time ago. Still are, maybe. I know Morgant puts great stock in Nimue — and it ain't just because she's Lady of the Lake now. I reckon Morgant figured she'd done all she could to persuade Arthur and it was up to Avalon and the new Lady to do what had to be done about Annis and the Sword. Morgant calls me to her a few days after she talked to Arthur and sends me off to Avalon. I don't know how she knew I was one of the Lady's . . . um . . . agents, but she did. Not much that woman don't know. Anyhow, when I brought Nimue the message, she right away calls up that bunch of young girls." Meredydd laughed and winked a watery blue eye at me. "Had a bit of a tussle with the Nine over you, young'n.

"For the life of me," she continued. "I don't understand why she sent girls and not women, and some not even Warriors. 'The Mother smiles on the young,' Nimue says. Well, it ain't for no mainlander to question the wisdom of the Lady of the Lake. I stayed on in Avalon for a while. Old Morgant the Merlin Falcon always rewards her friends and my reward was a month or so's leave up in Tref Briga with herself." Meredydd grinned and her face became almost soft. She looked at me. "Believe you know her. Big woman, red-headed as me."

"Ah," I said. "You're Briga's soul-friend. You

know, I always wanted to ask how you managed to tear her away from her cows."

"So much for Island tact," Elin said, but Meredydd just grinned some more.

"Had us a big time, Briga and me, compliments of Morgant. But last week I got word to come and fetch this Daughter. So here I am. And now let's start figuring out the route we ought to take up to Lystynes."

With that, she pulled out several large vellum pages and we spent the next hour or so examining them. When we had plotted our way, Meredydd poured herself some more wine and took the couch she'd occupied before. "Like I was saying, it's bad enough Arthur not wanting to avenge the Lady or Cormac, but him not wanting to bring back the Sword —" She shook her head. "It stands for the only thing he ever wanted — the union of the Realms. I remember them first battles against the English — Glein, then up and down the Dubglass. We'd whip 'em in one place and before they figured out what happened, we'd be hitting 'em fifty, sixty miles away. We was more like little brats robbing bees' nests than real warriors."

She chuckled and smiled, her eyes gazing into the past. " 'Course we'd been soldiers, most of us, almost since we was babies. But before Arthur we didn't fight the English no harder'n we fought each other. No one could unite us, not Ambrosius or Uther or even the emperor in Rome. At least not for long. Then Uther died and Arthur got elected king of Logres. It was like a new clan was born. We knew it from the day he took up Uther's sword. After that, Gwalchmei and Lancelot and Ceara Lyonesse and Bedwyr and all the rest of us — kings and clan-mothers, soldiers and singers — we ate and drank and wrestled and rode and sang together like kinfolk. Kai, too, good Christian though he was. Delighted, we was, and entertained and anxious, too. Full of hope and pride.

"Arthur was young. We all was, come to that. I can see him yet, opening his election games. Fairly dancing with pleasure. A skinny little fellow — shorter than me, even — and he didn't look more'n twelve, for all he was near twenty. All that beard and bulk, he got later. Bear, he's called now, but he sure didn't look like no bear as a boy, I can tell you. More like a pale yellow barn cat then. And just as tough. He could tear up a big brute like Bedwyr as easy as a tomcat can a wolfhound."

Meredydd gave a short nod of satisfaction at the comparison. And continued it. "A lot like a cat he was — aloof, cunning, and, come to think of it, cruel. You never knew what was in his mind. One minute he'd be frolicking and sweet and playful. The next he could look dopey with sleep. A minute later, he'd have his ears laid back, tail switching, ready to leap. Leap on an idea or a plan or, if somebody crossed him, even a man. I reckon that was his appeal. And the feeling you got that he was in charge of himself and everything around him."

I listened, fascinated. Elin, though, was no cat lover and had seen Arthur up close. She riffled through the maps, only half listening and then out of mere courtesy. Meredydd noticed her lack of attention and reached over and gave her a rap on the arm. "Watch a cat sometime, Healer. He looks like he's sound asleep or playing with his tail, but every second he's after knowing there's that mouse in the woodpile." Meredydd sighed. "I hope that's what Arthur's doing now — just trying to fool Annis or the English. Or somebody." She hoisted herself from the couch and said goodnight.

"But you didn't finish telling us about when Arthur became king," I called as she lurched out of the room.

When she didn't answer, I turned to Elin and said, "Well, looks like we'll have to find something else to do." I slurred the words, though, and missed completely when I tried to thrust my fingers through the neckline of her dress.

She pulled my hand to her breast. "Apparently, Arthur isn't the only one in the family with a weakness for the grape."

"Oh, it's not wine I want to taste now." Laughing, we ran through the marble hallways to bed.

In spite of the sweetness of Elin's love, I had trouble sleeping that night, so full of anticipation for our adventure was I. Just after midnight, I left our bed to prowl around the villa. An old hound bitch trailed after me. Looking up at the late autumn sky from the courtyard, I felt as if the whole world were spread out just for me. Elin joined me after awhile, and we sat gazing at the stars, not speaking, the dog asleep at our feet. If only happiness to that degree could last — or come again.

The trip north began easily enough. The weather held for several days and we made good time. Then it snowed — the wet heavy snow of autumn that comes silently in the night to cover the dying year.

We had taken shelter in a traveler's hut and the next morning I awoke to a splat of searing cold on my face. Then another and another. Elin stood outside the door, chunking snowballs at me. With a yelp I threw off my fur robe and lunged after her. She kept pelting me, but I finally chased her down to grind snow into her eyes, nose, and mouth. I stopped, though, when I looked at her with her dark hair spread out across the snow. And her lips, inviting mine, there in the cold, bright day. But duty called and we joined Meredydd where she stood with our mounts.

She led us through the white, anonymous world as easily as if it had been littered with Caesar's milestones. She found passes tucked tight and invisible between snowdrifts, located paths through moors the wind had swept clean, picked footing firm and sure in the icy muck of bogs.

When we sometimes stopped in villages or at farmsteads for the night, Meredydd paid for food and hospitality with stories of Camelot. I've no way of knowing whether or not they were true, even in outline, so embroidered were they with the highly colored threads of tales long told in the Celtic Realms. I recognized a story I'd once heard from a Spanish merchant: it had had nothing to do with Camelot.

As we drew closer to her brother's kingdom, Meredydd's stories began to show an increasing longing for that home. Her brother had recently taken a new wife, she told us one night as we huddled by the fire. King Pellam had long been widowed; the woman of his youth had died before her time and he mourned her past measure. But within the last year, loneliness defeated grief and Pellam had married again.

"I thought when he found a new woman, she'd be young," Meredydd said. "But he says he's got enough children to inherit his cattle and he didn't want to look like a silly old man who's bought him a young wife. 'Good enough,' I says when he wrote about it. 'Knowing him, he'll at least find a widow rich as he is and they'll strike such a bargain as'll fill their byres with half the hooves in Lystynes.' Wrong again. Pellam ups and marries the village midwife — a woman with three, maybe four cows, and hair whiter'n winter.

"I went to the wedding, mostly to find out who'd soon be wearing the purple in Lystynes, him being put away out of senility. But there he was, looking like a bristly young boar in rutting season, so bright was his eyes and smug his smile. And she — without a man these thirty years, and more used to wearing frayed shearling than Belgian linen — she stood next to him proud as if she had nine kings in her blood and nine princes in her belly."

Meredydd cut a large section of dried meat off the haunch we'd brought and washed it down with the last of Elin's estate-brewed beer. " 'Aha,' I says to myself, 'married him for his wealth, the wily old bitch. No more cold midnights burying afterbirth for you, eh, my lady? It'll be all fox fur and mulled cider now.' Wrong again. And I knew it the first time I saw them look at each other. That look — well, he's a happy man, my brother."

Meredydd stared into the fire for a moment. "And a settled one." She gave us a lopsided grin as if she'd said too much, and hied herself off to bed.

I glanced at Elin. She had seemed surprised by the droop of Meredydd's shoulders. But I knew then how Briga had been wooed away from her cows.

The next day we crossed into Lystynes. Meredydd had risen early and ridden ahead. Perhaps she was anxious to get home; perhaps she'd finally decided to give Elin and me some time alone. At any rate, we took good advantage of her absence and it was almost noon before we started out. Even then we were unwilling to be much separated and I rode pillion behind Elin, my face snug against her sweet-smelling hair. We had no trouble following Meredydd's tracks through the snow and soon we were on what was obviously King Pellam's high road.

It had begun to snow again when we caught up with her. She was standing at a crossroad. A little ways away, in the verge, her horse searched for something to nibble.

"Have you not been home in so long, you've forgot the way?" Elin called as we rode up.

Meredydd didn't answer; merely pointed down. A man lay there, naked and headless.

"English work, do you think?" Elin asked, dismounting.

"Maybe. But there's no English hereabouts. Or at least there never was before."

Elin looked around. "But, see, there's horse tracks. Lots of 'em."

"Could be bandits, but I don't think so — nor English. Something else."

Elin nodded.

We had set to work burying the man before I understood what Meredydd meant. The headless body at a crossroad . . . "Balin and —"

"Smart girl," Meredydd said as we lowered the body into the shallow grave we'd scraped out of the frozen ground.

We said the prayers for the dead and rode on, silent as the snow that lay thick over Pellam's land.

After we found the second body — headless, too, and at a crossroad — we began to hurry. Meredydd pushed her horse hard against the snowdrifts and fast across the wind-swept spots. When night came she stopped only because of the beast's exhaustion; the darkness meant nothing to her, so well did she know the way. Elin and I kept up the pace as best we could but eventually we fell far behind, to again follow her tracks.

We passed a few farms, snow-hidden and empty of people and animals. In all that great plain, there seemed to be no life. Only the endless, unbroken snow, lying on the land like the shroud on a corpse.

At last we saw the villa. And the birds — scavengers making slow loops high above the walls. A lone figure stood before the open gates; she seemed as frozen as the landscape. Elin and I spurred the horses hard up the hill, past its wheatfields and the vineyard that clung to its slope. Above, we could see the roofs of the house and its barns and shops and bath.

We dismounted and tied the horses at the gate. Inside the villa's walls — where there should have been the honking of geese, the warning barks of dogs, the shouts and laughter of slaves; where there should have been a barnyard stinking and slick with churned mud and manure — there was only snow, smooth, undisturbed.

The courtyard, too, was empty and snow-filled,

and its fountain still, icicles clinging to the veranda eaves. The front door of the house stood open, threshold covered with drifted snow. The room beyond was also empty. Save for a grey-haired woman lying face down on the mosaicked floor.

The three of us stood staring at her for several moments before Meredydd turned her over. Her throat had been cut. One swipe of a sharp blade had sliced through nearly to the backbone. It was a neat job, the work of an expert swordsman. Only the huge splotch of dried blood was messy.

Meredydd took the dead woman into her arms and held her for a long time before she finally said, "This is Gwladys. She was born the same day as me. We sucked the same tit. We played together when we was children and she was the first woman I knew. When I came of age, my father gave her to me, along with her husband and her children. I freed them. Signed the manumission papers right here in this room."

She looked up at Elin and me, her eyes gone blank. We only stared back, dumb.

When we had taken in the situation — silent farm, empty house, slaughtered freedwoman — our glances raised from the grieving Meredydd to the closed doors that led to the rest of the house. Elin slipped her sword from its sheath and walked to a door and kicked it open. But for its ornate furniture, the room beyond was empty.

Together, we opened the other door. Inside, it was as dark as everything else. But its smell told us what the darkness hid.

"Don't go in yet," Elin whispered to me, not wanting to further alarm the still-shocked Meredydd.

"I'll get something to use as a torch." And she hurried off to the farmyard.

I stared into the room, trying to accustom my eyes to its dimness. The small light from the door showed little, but I could see what looked like — "Sacks of wheat, that's all," I said, stupid with relief.

When Elin returned with the torch, we went in. There was no wheat in that room.

Chapter Ten

Human bodies lay on the floor, on the couches, heaped in the corners, stretched out, crumpled, sprawled, tossed on top of each other. There are no words to describe that room. Nor to tell of the scream we heard from behind us. It blasted me out of my own horror — a sound like I thought no human or animal could ever make, nor like any from the Otherworld. We turned. Meredydd stood in the door frame.

She was staring down at a man's severed arm, which lay almost at our feet. On its forefinger was an immense amethyst ring, a royal ring. Elin had the sense to wheel Meredydd around and, with the butt of her sword, knock her cold. "You, you get out of there," she yelled at me as she lowered Meredydd to the vestibule floor. And I did.

The two of us stood in the vestibule, shivering with cold and fear and horror, wondering what to do.

"We've got to get those people out of that room and decently buried," I said, voice thick. "But there must be a couple of dozen of them and it's winter and there's no one here to wash them and shroud them and sing their funeral songs." I was frightened and confused and ready to burst into tears. We both were.

And why not? We were hardly more than children, confronted with a crime of such proportions we could barely comprehend it. Yes, we were trained as soldiers and Elin as a physician. She had seen a fair amount of combat, but, I tell you, what she had seen on battlefields, and what I would see, was far more comprehensible than that dark room full of death.

"We'll need help," I said at last. "Pellam's clansmen must live nearby. And the whole country can't be dead." I looked at Elin. "Can they?"

We were finally able to lead Meredydd from the house. Elin brushed the snow off a stone bench in the courtyard, where we sat Meredydd down. She refused the narcotic Elin offered from her Healer's pack, but we got enough wine into her to stop her shaking. It took longer, though, to find out how to get to the nearest clansman, for Meredydd had already begun the ritual of mourning. She threw her cloak over her head and ripped open her tunic. We did not try to stop her as she clawed her face and tore at her breasts. But when she went for her eyes, Elin caught her in a strong bear hug.

When her first grief had spent itself, Meredydd gave us directions to her brothers and Elin and I drew straws to see which would go. Elin won. After a quick kiss, she leaped on her horse and was off. I sat in the cold listening to the high, thin wail of Meredydd's keen. She no longer appeared to want to mutilate herself, so, after awhile, I left her and wandered about in the flat grey of the winter afternoon.

All fear seemed to have gone from me, nor did I feel surprise or even much compassion when, behind a haystack, I came across two more bodies, young boys cut down with the wooden hayforks still in their hands. As I was brushing the snow off them, I heard a sound — inside the hay mound. I drew my sword and began to prod it.

In a few minutes, a girl of about thirteen emerged. I sheathed the sword and held out my hand, explaining that the danger was past. She jumped back, stumbling over a snow-covered bucket. She was fair-haired, of medium height, dressed in the half-tunic of a house slave. The shiny pink of an old burn blotched one side of her face from mouth to hairline. It pulled down the corner of her eye, giving her a feral look, emphasized just then by fear — her lips curled over her teeth like a cornered animal's. I believe she would have fought me if I'd tried to touch her.

I offered a stick of dried meat. After a moment's hesitation, she snatched it and gobbled it down

eagerly. When she'd finished, she let me take her to
the barn, out of the wind and cold. There, I sat
down on a block of wood that lay on the floor, but
the girl crouched in a corner, huddled in her wool
cloak, eyes downcast. I talked to her in a quiet
voice, explaining who I was in both British and
Irish. She showed no understanding of either until I
mentioned Pellam's new queen.

"Dead, her?" she asked and raised her gaze to
the level of my chest.

"With the others," I answered.

She wept, silently at first, then in gasps, then in
screams wild as a winter storm. I tried to comfort
her by putting my arms around her, but she flung
me away with surprising strength. When eventually
she grew calm, I offered wine from my flask. After
she drank in noisy gulps, she began to talk.

She told me she was an English slave named
Godgyth, and only recently come to Pellam's villa as
part of a wedding gift from the King of Domnonia.
Although she could understand British well enough,
she apparently spoke only the peculiar jargon of
slaves — part Celtic, part English, and sounding like
no dialect of either. I had some difficulty with it at
first (Elin's slaves spoke good British), but, after
awhile and with the addition of gestures, I picked up
enough to understand.

Her story went like this: Several days before, the
villa had been at its business when a young man
carrying the Dragon Shield rode in, along with two
or three companions. Apparently, the guards at the
gate knew him, or were sufficiently awed by the
Dragon Shield; the men were admitted without
difficulty and welcomed warmly by Pellam and his

family. A feast was laid, which Godgyth helped prepare.

About midday she was sent to the farmyard with bread and buttermilk for the farmhands' noon meal. She was dipping out the buttermilk for two lads who had been pulling hay down from the stack when they heard screams from the villa. They ran around to the other side of the stack. There, through the thick fog that had set in, they saw a swarm of soldiers chopping down everyone and everything — people, dogs, even the fowl in their pens. Godgyth dived into the haystack.

"Where were Pellam's warriors?" I asked. "Why didn't they protect you?"

"No warrior. Alone us. Friends hayforks use." She gestured toward the haystack and the two bodies. "No warrior come help." Again she burst into tears.

Godgyth had stayed in the stack, terrified and hardly daring to breathe as she listened to the sounds of murder. Finally, the screaming stopped; then she could hear orders being barked and grunts and curses as the dead were removed from the farmyard.

"Why didn't they take the two boys?" I asked. "Or search the haystack?" Godgyth didn't know, but she said the noises ended suddenly. "Whistle come. Then gone." Even so, she had stayed hidden until I came along.

By the Mother, I thought, what could have happened? How could Pellam's warband have let its king and his household die alone? As I was pondering, the girl began to shriek again: horses were approaching. Slowly, I opened the hut door a crack and peeked out. It was Elin, with Pellam's grim-faced clansmen.

We buried Pellam and his household in the pigsty. It was the only place were the earth was not completely frozen. "How ignoble," Elin said as we laid the royal family in the bottom of the reeking trench.

"Meredydd says it's not so awful," I babbled. "She says her clan is descended from the boar."

"Still!" Elin spat. By then her horror had passed and she was angry, a cold anger that froze her mouth into a straight line and turned her eyes the color of dirty ice.

We placed Pellam and his new queen together. They had died that way, I think. We found them at the bottom of that terrible heap of bodies, her arms around him, his remaining hand resting on her white head. Next to them we put the King's other sister and her grandson, a child of about three. The rest, slaves and freedmen, were buried in a vast common grave.

We did not find the remains of any warriors.

The funeral lasted for only two days, cut short by the snow and lack of mourners. There were no games, no song-fests, only the howl of the wind and the shouts of angry, drunken men. The day afterward, Meredydd formally refused the throne of Lystynes, telling the clan it belonged to one or the other of Pellam's sons. Then she declared blood feud and began gathering up troops to march against Balin.

"You two can stay or come. It makes no difference to me," she told Elin and me, her voice a dark growl. "The Lady may have her own plan when she hears of this, but I renounce my vows to her. My clan comes first now. If you decide to join us, you must put yourself in my service and no other."

Without hesitation, Elin knelt down before Meredydd. "I, Elin, elected Queen of Calchvynydd, declare blood feud against Balin of Reged and his allies. I place myself, my domain, and my clan at your disposal. I swear this by all the gods." And she kissed Meredydd's breast.

The rightness of Meredydd's cause was without question and everything in me cried out for vengeance. But I was a servant of the Mother, bound to follow the orders of the Lady. Only, events had overtaken those instructions and no others would be forthcoming for I knew not how long. I didn't want to stay in that place of death to await new orders and I certainly didn't want to be without Elin. It was the first time in my life that I'd been faced with such a predicament.

I wandered away from the council circle. It had snowed again in the night, covering Pellam's villa and his land with a glittering white pall. For an hour or so, I pushed the snow, so bright I could barely look at it, covering the ground with the elaborate linked designs I had learned in childhood: some knotwork, a few two-coiled spirals (I never could manage three coils), and an interlaced dragon, crude but big.

By the time I went back inside, I knew I would go north with Elin and Meredydd. Surely, I reasoned, Avalon's interests in this matter coincided with Meredydd's. It didn't seem to me that this was the kind of tribal self-interest I'd been taught was the weakness of our race. It was, of course, but I, too, am a Celt.

"And as for the snow," Meredydd was saying when I came into the hall, "the better to track him through." Her equanimity had returned in some measure, but the shock of the massacre had taken the twinkle from her eye. Nor did she smile anymore. She thought only of Balin. And Annis.

"She's behind this. That's obvious, even if she didn't take no heads," she said, and spat into the fire. The spittle hissed against the grate.

While we waited for Meredydd to raise her army — it took several weeks — we settled into one of Pellam's smaller villas, which had been inhabited by its overseer. Meredydd's nephews sent provisions and some of their house slaves to make us comfortable.

There's an old saying that it's a cold breakfast after a massacre. And, sure, it is, but Elin and I ate it anyway — and drank and slept and made love. For a long time, we fled into our senses. It was easy enough; there were few people and no duties to disturb us. When she was not in council, Meredydd retreated to an upstairs room with her maps and a succession of ale barrels. The slaves kept their distance. Except for the girl, Godgyth, who began to follow me around.

She was a pathetic little thing, with her pale, scarred face and hazy blue eyes, but anxious to please. At table, I had only to reach for the wine bottle for her to snatch it up and fill my drinking-cup. In the evening, unasked, she warmed our bed with a flannel-covered brick. When I thanked her — I wasn't used to slaves — she answered with downcast eyes and a hand to her forelock. Elin said next she'd be sleeping at the foot of our bed.

I felt sorry for her. She was alone, her friends dead, and at the mercy of the slavemaster. Besides, she hadn't gotten over the terror she'd known as she lay hidden in that haystack. She still jumped at every strange noise and, once, went screaming into the fields at the sudden yowl of a pair of cats. Gradually, though, she began to feel more secure and we sometimes talked as she drew our baths or laid out our clothes (I'd found out how easy it is to be waited on).

At about this time, one of Meredydd's grand-nephews broke his neck when his horse bolted at the shadow of a bird on the snow. His father, knowing Elin was an Avalon-trained healer, prevailed on her to come to his estate and treat the boy. We decided I wouldn't join her; that house was already in turmoil enough.

While she was gone, I read and talked to Meredydd a little but mostly moped, missing Elin. One evening, as I sat in my bedroom trying to amuse myself with the only book in the villa, a volume of Cicero's duller speeches, Godgyth came in with a beaker of hot wine. As she bent to pour, I reached out and touched the scar that blotched her face from eye to mouth. "How came you by this?"

She leaped back and for a moment there came again the feral look I'd seen in the farmyard. "An accident?" I went on. "It must have hurt."

She turned away, a little smile playing at the corners of her mouth.

I let the matter drop, not wanting to cause her the pain of memory. But a day or so later, I found her gazing into a looking-glass, her hand to the scar. There were tears in her eyes. "So ugly makes," she said and threw down the glass. "Irisher this do. Ram me, make *fader* watch, then this do."

The Irish slavers had caught the people of her village at harvest. They killed the old ones, leaving their bodies to rot in the fields with the half-reaped grain. The rest — men, women, children — they herded into stockpens, out of which they would choose the strongest and handsomest. The Irish, it seemed, preferred their slaves good-looking. Godgyth and her family spent the night there, huddling in each others' arms and listening to the Irish — there were several dozen of them — getting drunk on the villagers' mead.

In the morning, the praying, weeping people, arms bound behind them, were lined up at spear-point. A big, dark-haired man dressed in a badger-skin cloak and wearing a torque of twisted wire came to make the selection. "This — this — not this —" he would say as he moved along the line of English. Those of whom he said "this" were pushed back in the pen. The others, including Godgyth's mother, were led away at the end of ropes, like dogs.

He stood for a long time before Godgyth and her father, eyeing Godgyth. Then he reached out and ripped open the front of her dress, exposing her just forming breasts. *"Fader,* he jump on Irisher."

Her father charged, head down. The other slavers were on him immediately, of course, but not before he'd smashed the Irishman to the ground and broken a couple of his teeth. The Irishman picked himself up and put his hand to this mouth. He looked at the blood on his fingers, then wiped it off on his stiff fur cloak. Meanwhile, the men holding Godgyth's still-struggling father waited to see how their chief wanted to deal with him. Godgyth begged for his life.

But it was not her father the big Irishman wanted. He stripped Godgyth naked, threw her down, and raped her. When he'd finished, he offered her to three or four of the other slavers. Godgyth could not remember how long it went on. After awhile, she no longer felt the agony between her legs or heard the screams of the villagers as they pleaded with the Irish to stop. Nor did she know what happened to her father; she'd been unconscious when the chief threw her back in the pen. Later, the other English told her he'd been taken away. She assumed he was dead.

On the voyage back to Ireland, the chief kept her for his personal use and that of a few of his favorites among the slavers. Once, on the bank of a creek where they'd drawn up their boats and cargo for the night, she tried to resist. He held her head in the fire. It hurt less than being raped, she said. The worst of it was the smell of her own roasting flesh. The burn took a long time to heal and, by then, she was damaged goods. But the chief, that superb merchant, struck a fine bargain with the King of Domnonia: "Me for a set of chessmen. Walnut." She said it with a tinkling laugh.

After that, she talked more often, until we chattered together like old section-mates, though, of course, she was just a child. I tried to tell her about my love for Elin, but she didn't seem to understand.

164

However, she did show great interest in Avalon and I was homesick enough to tell her all about it, even bragging a bit about how I'd been chosen to look for Balin so that the Lady's death could be avenged.

"This Annis," she asked when I'd finished. "She like goddess?"

"Well —"

"Like *waelcyrge? Waelcyrge* is —"

I told her I knew what a *waelcyrge* was. "Annis is the sister of the Mother. There are three sisters, actually. The Mother, Annis, and Babd. They share such things as snow and the sea, but it's the Mother who brings flowers, fruit, life to us and our lands. She gives us our flesh," I explained. "Babd stirs the Cauldron from which we draw wisdom and inspiration and enlightenment. Some even say that those who drink from it can change the future. Annis, though, is the enemy of the other two. She wants all the world for herself and she leads a warband called the Grey Host."

"Who follow such a one?" Godgyth said, throwing her hands up in horror.

I struggled to explain — that Annis stole the souls of those whose heads she captured and turned them against even their own brothers — and against the Mother.

"Why you not find? Kill?"

"Her fortress is way up at the top of the world and anyway her troops don't travel on foot or horse. They fly. She turns them into starlings."

Godgyth gave me a disgusted look. It was clear she thought I was toying with her, playing on her credulity as a mere slave and foreigner. I changed the subject. "Come," I said. "It's a nice day. I'll show you how to use a sling. Then you'll be able to protect yourself better."

She proved utterly inept with the sling; she couldn't keep a stone in long enough to get it over her head. But we continued our conversations anyway — about slave life, Avalon, the weather, everything, anything — even after Elin came back.

I saw her ride up and ran immediately to the stables; Elin always put away her own horse. I tore at the doeskin riding trousers before her feet even touched the floor, ripping away the button at the waist so that she stepped out of them as we sank into the warm straw. When we were momentarily satisfied, we dressed and went to our room in the villa, where we began the whole ritual of rut once, no, many times more.

In the morning, I finally thought to ask about the boy. "He'll live," Elin said. "Though he may wish Arawn had taken him to the Otherworld. I doubt he'll walk again." I waited for her to say more, but, of course, she didn't.

Godgyth came in with breakfast and stayed while we ate, chattering blithely on about the new batch of kittens out in the byre. When she'd cleared away the dishes and gone back to the kitchen, Elin said, "Well, I see you two have become fine friends in my absence." She sounded somewhat aggrieved.

"She's rather a sweet little thing," I mumbled into Elin's left breast which I was then beginning to give renewed attention.

Elin made a vulgar noise.

"Are you jealous, then?" I asked, running my

166

tongue around the nipple pink and puckered as a wild strawberry.

"Of course not." She pushed me away and pulled up the sheepskin blanket. "Godgyth's a *slave*. And *you're* a Daughter of Avalon."

I didn't know whether to laugh or cry. So I teased. "You didn't seem to mind tupping the children of slaves when you were on the Island. Whole flocks of them, from what I've heard. And I know for a fact that you and Branwen — Anyway, I might very well have been born a slave myself."

She tossed the sheepskin away and sat naked on the side of the bed. "You're a queen's child and a king's. Or at least a warrior's."

"Maybe," I answered. "Oh, Elin, don't be jealous. It's silly and childish. Besides, she's only a little girl."

She turned and pointed a finger at me. "I'm not jealous. Maybe you're the one who should be, though. Haven't you noticed the way she looks at me?"

I did laugh then and mumbled something about putting a bucket over her handsome head. She continued to point at me.

"It's just that I don't like that creature. Always sneaking around with those slitty eyes and that nasty little smile. And she makes fun of you behind your back. I've heard her with the other slaves. I understand English, you know."

I grabbed her finger, twisting and biting it. "Come back under the covers and make different use of this thing." She did, but, of course, it didn't solve the problem of Godgyth.

One day shortly after this conversation, Godgyth

and I were in one of the villa's ornate living rooms. Elin had gone to talk to Meredydd about the extended break in the weather and I was practicing the English which Godgyth had begun to teach me. (Elin had adamantly refused to teach me. "I'm no damned tutor.")

"The Queen don't like me, does she?" she said suddenly in English just as I was in the midst of naming the pieces of furniture.

"The Queen? Oh, you mean Elin. Well... Surely there must be another word for *chair*. *Stool* is a downright ugly sound for something so beautiful." The chair I pointed at was gilded mahogany.

"She don't." Godgyth chewed her lip as she spoke.

"No," I said in English. "She don't." There was no point in lying.

"Do you want me to go away, then?"

I was utterly confounded. "Why, for the Mother?"

"Because she's your beloved and a queen."

"What has that to do with whether or not you stay with us?"

Godgyth frowned and said, "She won't want it."

"Well, *I* do. And, besides, where else could you go?"

Suddenly, she dropped to her knees in front of me and pressed my hand to her lips. "Thank you," she said and wept.

I was terribly embarrassed, and got her stopped as soon as I could, but I was also terribly moved. When I told Elin what had happened, she said, "Nothing but a slave trick, Argante. Don't let her flatter you. You'll end up the servant and she the mistress."

"But we're neither. We're friends!"

At last the preparations for our journey were finished. The army Meredydd had finally managed to raise was small and ragtag — a few dozen, at most, of her clan and their bondsmen. But the cry had gone forth and more would follow in the spring, from Calchvynydd, from Scathach in Scotland, perhaps from Camelot and Avalon. Meredydd pronounced herself satisfied.

The night before we were to leave, she and her kinsmen joined Elin and me for supper. We drank up the last of the villa's wine and were well into the ale when I drew a deep breath and said, "Godgyth will be coming with us."

"Wha-a-t?" Elin demanded with elaborate disgust.

"I've arranged it with Meredydd. Godgyth's her property now and she says what's another slave more or less." I looked at Meredydd, who shrugged assent. "And, remember, Godgyth's the only one who knows what these killers look like."

It wasn't quite the truth, but by then I'd made up my mind to get Godgyth to Avalon, even if I had to buy her.

"We all know Balin," Elin pointed out, setting her ale cup down with a thump.

"But she's seen the rest. Don't you want to be able to take exact revenge?"

Meredydd stood up then and said, "If they're with Balin, that's good enough for me." She drew a finger across her throat. "Bring the girl or leave her. I don't care." She left the dining room, taking her nephews and her ale with her.

Elin and I argued on until finally she shook her

head and went silent. We sat staring into the congealed remains of roast chicken until it was time to go to bed.

Godgyth went north with us.

Although I very nearly had second thoughts when I saw the pack she intended to carry. It was big enough to have made the Morrigan herself proud. "You can't take all that," I told her.

"But, Madam — Argante, I mean. It's clothes, cosmetics. Oils to dress your hair, perfume. You'll want to stay beautiful for *her*."

Elin was loading a pack mule nearby and I heard her snicker. I explained that we were going to war, not to a feast.

"Even so, Madam. But —"

"That's right, Godgyth," Elin called. "You explain cosmetics to Argante. And to the rest of the Daughters when you get to Avalon. You'll be most popular."

"Shut up! Both of you. Godgyth, get rid of that stuff. Now!"

The girl scrambled back into the house while I glowered at Elin. She returned to the mule, grinning and humming the while. Godgyth came back with a much smaller sack, though it, too, bulged generously.

Chapter Eleven

We made remarkably good time. The weather stayed cold but clear and Meredydd picked a safe course. Before long we were in the mountains. I won't go into detail about the month we spent crawling through them. Suffice to say it was more exhausting than exciting. In plain fact, it was boring. The people in whose farmsteads and hill forts we stayed were as dull as bear and badger asleep in their dens. Our only adventures came the time two pack mules fell down a crevice and when one of the bondsmen lost his mind and tried to eat his brother's elbow.

We were nearing Balin's *dun* — Meredydd reckoned we were within a week of it — when the sky suddenly darkened and we could smell snow on the air. So quickly did the storm come up that we only just had time to reach the next *dun* before it struck.

This fort was small; its rampart enclosed only an acre or two. Nothing like the ones I've seen in other parts of Britain or in Gaul. But it was well-protected, the hill it sat atop so steep and craggy that an attacker would have no choice but to wind between its stone rings for half a mile, his shieldless side exposed to its summit all the way. We ourselves had to lead our mounts up that path, and even then the horses slipped in its tight twists and icy mud. On the hill's top was a thick rock rampart and heavily timbered gate.

But the gate was broken and whole sections of the rampart lacked their wooden palisade. We called out, begging hospitality. The only answer was the howl of the wind. Inside, the hall and outbuildings in which we finally took shelter were solid, but no one peopled them and their thatched roofs were rotten and fallen. It had been a prince's court, we concluded from the quality of the furnishings. But who he was and where he'd gone, we couldn't guess: the wind had swept long through those empty rooms.

Fortunately, we didn't have to spend the storm among the roofless walls, huddled under leather lean-tos. The *dun* had the usual rooms carved into its rampart and we were able to sleep warm and dry, with our animals properly stabled. Still, the place made me uneasy.

Now, I'm a child of the day, born well after dawn, and so lack any of the night child's eerie gifts. But, for once in my life, the second sight was near on me. I fidgeted and tossed and, according to Elin, groaned the night through. Until the shouts of our terrified watch informed us that at the foot of the hill there stood an immense army.

Annis's Grey Host! The filthy stink of them filled our noses as Elin, Meredydd, Godgyth, and I looked down from the rampart.

"Some of Pellam's men are down there," Meredydd said in a toneless voice. "Lads I grew up with, drank with. The Hag's men now." She turned away, spat out a sharp curse, and went off to inspect our supplies.

"She couldn't recognize any of them, could she?" I whispered to Elin.

"Even their gods couldn't recognize them," Godgyth said. She was probably right. Grey Ones have the bodies of warriors, fitted out in the ordinary way — leather cuirasses; ash-shafted spears; long, white-washed shields; Spanish swords. It's their heads — the repository of the soul — that make you sick. They're bloated, featureless; grey and glutinous as the faces of the long-drowned.

"Uch," I said with a shudder.

"That's what happens when Annis or her . . . things take your head," Elin muttered. "You die but you don't." She pulled at her lower lip. "Come on, we'd better get busy. They're not going to stay down there forever, even if Annis doesn't seem to be around." She put her arm around me. "And don't look so scared. We've got the advantage of height and with the food we've got in our bags, we'll be able to hold out for a while. Then maybe we can find a way to break through or maybe Scathach or even Arthur will come." She seemed darkly excited at the prospect of battle and her hand held not a Healer's pouch but a sword.

I sent Godgyth to check on the horses tethered in the shelter of a crumbling barn on the far side of the *dun*. She had not yet returned when suddenly the wind came up, bringing with it a combination of snow and ice. Its screaming slash brought us all to a blind standstill. We could but hide in our cloaks, creep behind a wall, and pray (something I'd already been doing a lot of anyway). The only solace was that if we were paralyzed, so was the enemy.

When finally the storm slacked off, I peeked out of my not-very-warm hood to see, instead of snow, a flock of starlings wheeling on the wind. They settled on the ramparts, a dozen, two dozen. More and more until the rock was black with them. I felt sick. It was the way the Grey Host traveled — in great, shrieking clouds of starlings.

We had just enough time to form a battle-square, in hopes that in the snow our white-washed shields might make a rampart barely visible to the enemy, our spears an iron hedge. Because I was an inexperienced fighter, Meredydd positioned me in the middle. But the press of those behind thrust me forward and I had no choice but to stumble into the killing-zone. I soon found that battle is not writhing, faceless mass against faceless mass; it is a collection of individual, very personal murders. (Let go of any legends you might have heard — Grey Ones die in battle. In fact, they begin to rot even as they fall!)

After awhile — I don't know whether it was an hour or a day — I found myself next to Elin and Meredydd. Elin worked in close; her leather cuirass was covered with the stinking green slime that flows out of Grey Ones instead of blood. Meredydd, on the other hand, was a wily fighter, feinting and thrusting with an uneven motion that went counter to the steady rhythm of her cursing. As for me, the fighting was too close for my sling to be of any use and I've always been a poor swordswoman. I did the best I could.

Our line was spread out and thinning fast when suddenly the Grey Ones went still as the corpses they should have been. The storm abated. A dark figure pushed forward.

It was Balin the Brute himself. He stood before Meredydd, brandishing Arthur's sword and a yellow-toothed grin. In the cold air his breath steamed as he shouted out a battle-boast.

From his belt dangled the head of the Lady of the Lake.

Then he smashed his sword — Arthur's steel sword, I saw — down through the hide of Meredydd's shield, breaking it but missing Meredydd. I moved forward to help. Elin pulled me back. "It's a sword-pact now," she said as she stripped the shield off her arm, ready to hand it to Meredydd when she could.

Balin was strong, but slow, and Arthur's sword was of the long, Celtic kind, not as efficient as Meredydd's short Spanish weapon. Meredydd parried it once, then ducked under its wide sweep to slash

Balin's unprotected right leg. The cut went deep in, just above the knee. It rocked Balin backward long enough for Meredydd to grab the shield that Elin held out. They circled for a while, until a feint by Meredydd drew Balin in close. Their shields came together with a crash and locked. Balin pulled his blade back to gain another wide sweep. As he did, the shorter Meredydd drove hers upward, past Balin's immobile shield, and into his neck. He fell, clutching at the rush of blood where his throat had been.

Meredydd threw down her own weapon and caught up the steel sword. In almost the same motion, she chopped through the hank of hair that fastened Lile's head to Balin's belt. The Grey Ones made no move, their dull eyes on the dying Balin, swords still at their sides.

"Run, you two," Meredydd yelled at Elin and me. "To the horses, if you can. If not, the gate. Take this with you." She flung Lile's head at us. She used the hair as a handle and some of it stayed in her fist.

The head itself fell into a puddle. Elin scooped it up on the bounce. "This is yours," she said, jamming it into my ribs and very nearly knocking the breath out of me. Then she joined Meredydd, dispatching one of the Grey Ones before they fully threw off their stupor.

I rolled Lile's head — it lacked an ear, I noticed — tight into my cloak, which I threw over my right shoulder and pinned under my shield arm with the blue penannular of Avalon. It formed an awkward lump under my breast, but the shield protected it, and I was soon ready to get back to the Grey Ones.

Just then, though, the storm took up again and

before I could move, the world disappeared. I tried to follow the sounds of battle, but they evaporated into the howl of the wind. At last I heard a blast of a horn. It was somewhat distant, but I turned toward it. The snow made for hard going. I stumbled, slipped, fell. Inside my head, a sun burst.

When I came around, the snow had drifted a little and I lay not far from one of the broken sections of rampart. I could hear the battle, raging still but on the other side of the *dun*.

Godgyth was leaning over me, reaching for Lile's head. It was still tucked into my cloak and the pouch of Island dirt was still at my belt. My shield lay next to me, but sword and sling were gone.

"I'll be having that," Godgyth said in British as her fingers touched the cloak.

I pulled back, brushing her hand away. "Only a Daughter may touch it," I said, trying not to sound too harsh.

She made a grab then, which I only fended off by jumping up and backing away, cloak pressed against me. My head hurt and I felt sick, but when Godgyth looked up from where she still knelt, I could see that the scar that had blotched her face was gone. In the air was the smell of burnt cloves.

"Godgyth?" My voice was a whisper.

She laughed. It was like the sound of a bell. "There was never any Godgyth, my dear. Only me. Too bad you have no magic. It would have let you see what was in front of your eyes." She stood up.

I knew what was before them now. Annis.

I backed away another few yards. But the rampart wall stopped me. I could feel the rough, uneven rock cutting into my back.

"Hand me what you have in your cloak," she said, holding out her hand and still smiling. "Give it to me and I'll not harm you. No more than I did after you let my hare be killed or when you angered the pig. And who got you out of that English village?"

Again there came the sound of a horn. It was at the base of the *dun*. Annis lowered her hand. "It seems Scathach has arrived. I should have buried her and her whole army before they ever left Scotland." Her smile twisted into a snarl as she barked out an order. Behind her, from out of the thick swirl of snow that obscured the rest of the *dun*, appeared a phalanx of Grey Ones.

Then I yelled, screamed, shrieked for help. Surely Elin and Meredydd would come. But they were too busy. I could hear Meredydd's big braying voice rallying her clansmen and Elin's wolf-howl of a battle cry.

When finally I hushed, Annis smiled again. "Ought the Pendragon's daughter wail so? Perhaps it's wrong about you I've been all these years. Perhaps you're not his child." She smoothed back her pale gold hair. "Little matter now. You've served your purpose. I'll soon rule in Avalon." She again extended her hand. "As soon as I have the Lady's head."

I glanced past her at the still line of Grey Ones. Their eyes reminded me of milk gone sour. "Purpose?" I mumbled, putting a hand out behind me to grope at the rough wall.

"But then again maybe you are his daughter. He's also a great one for stalling. Your purpose? Use that intellect Claudia has made you so proud of."

While she spoke she moved toward me, slowly, and with her hand still thrust out. The Grey Ones moved with her.

Any intellect I might have had was at that moment focused on saving my hide.

"You were trying so hard to impress a slave girl with your own glory and other people's plans that —"

Another blast on the horn and battle shouts from below. Scathach and her troops were moving up the hill. As the horn blast came, I scrambled up onto the top of the rampart.

"Ah, my dear. Now what good could that possibly do? You'll win no glory there."

What good indeed? Behind me were Annis and her Grey Ones. In front, I could barely see Scathach's troops through the snow and down a four-hundred-foot slope criss-crossed with rock walls. Furthermore, I was unarmed. All I had for protection was Lile's head, still wrapped in the cloak wound around me. Why couldn't it be like the severed head of Bran and speak to the living? And tell me what to do now!

A hard gust of wind pushed at me and, as I threw my hands out to keep my balance, I brushed against the pouch of Island dirt at my waist. 'Concentrate, girl. . .' I could almost hear old Cerridwen yelling at me. 'Believe yourself flying, believe in the wind against your wings.' Do it, I told myself. Change yourself into a bird and fly out of here. It's only a knack.

A spear, two, spurted past my ear.

I yanked my cloak free from around me and caught the ends together, shaking Lile's head loose in the fold. Then I swung the cloak in wide circles. And let one end go. Lile's head shot out of the makeshift sling. As it sailed down the slope toward Scathach, the sun appeared.

Immediately I lost my footing on the rampart's narrow top and fell — to roll twenty, thirty yards through ice and snow and mud until the wall of one of the fort's rings stopped me. I hit with a thump and lay next to it, panting and too terrified to get up. But, before long, there was a shout from the rampart and I looked up to see a grinning Elin peering over its top.

The storm had moved off, and with it, the Grey Host.

As far as I could tell, no one but me had seen Annis. I thought no one would believe me. I left her out of my explanation of why I'd thrown Lile's head, saying only that I'd been surrounded by a troop of Grey Ones. Indeed, I counted myself lucky that those Grey Ones at the wall had been seen by Meredydd and her clansmen. They killed a few before the rest rose as starlings and flew after the retreating storm. Even so, there was a good bit of consternation in Scathach's army about the condition of Lile's head after its inglorious descent from the top of the *dun*. And mutterings about sacrilege.

But when Scathach heard my story, she said, "If Avalon wants lily-handed maidens, it best turn Christian and be done. 'Pears to me the chit did what she had to. It's honor she should be getting now, not blame." With that, the squat old queen stumped off to help Meredydd break open a barrel of ale. And there were no more complaints. Scathach's poet even made a song about me. But I heard much later that Branwen had been especially distressed.

However, she greeted me warmly enough, though scarcely with Faencha's massive delight. "Holy Mother," Faencha shouted as she yanked me into her dark arms. "We've been scared you were milking Arawn's cows in the Otherworld!" Then she and Branwen and I hugged and kissed and cried. The occasion brought a slap on the back from the Hound. After Branwen led us in prayer of thanksgiving and we'd helped bury the dead, we settled down with a small cask of wine to share our adventures. (Elin was still seeing to the wounded.)

The three of them had gotten to Scathach's fortress long before hard winter and remained there until Meredydd's messenger arrived, "More icicle than man," Branwen said. "But I, for one, was glad to have an excuse to leave Scathach's. A cold, barren rock and nothing but ice as far as the eye could see." She shivered down into her fur-lined cloak.

"I liked it, myself," Faencha said. "Scathach's a great warrior and —"

"And she's got a willing daughter," the Hound said with a smirk.

"Maybe we'd better get the tent up," Branwen broke in. "Argante can tell us what happened to her while we're working."

I told my story, carefully leaving out any mention of Godgyth. Or Annis. When the six-trooper Roman tent was up, Branwen assigned me my place in it. I told her I now slept with Elin.

Faencha looked up from where she was tightening a guy-rope. "You do?"

"Oh, ho! It's that way, is it?" the Hound said, smirking again. "Mmmmm. A bit of slap and tickle for our hero."

Without warning, Faencha wheeled on the Hound, catching her by a scruff of tunic and shaking her so hard her teeth clattered. "What kind of talk is that?" she snarled into the Hound's surprised face.

"Jealous are you?" the Hound retorted.

Branwen threw down her hammer and pulled the two apart. "None of this now. There'll be no fighting while I'm in charge." She ran a hand through her forelock and shook her head.

Faencha went back to the guy-rope, her face hidden. The Hound, who continued to smirk, elaborately adjusted her tunic.

"Go to her, then," Branwen said to me with a smile. "It's nobody's business but yours." She turned her centurion's glower back to the others. "As for you two —"

I left in a hurry.

Scathach, meanwhile, had dispatched messengers to Lystynes, Calchvynydd, and Avalon. The one she sent to Camelot carried with her both Arthur's sword and Balin's head. The Sword was unceremoniously wrapped in a rough piece of undyed wool, but Balin's head had the blue seal of Avalon knotted into its blood-matted hair. "That ought to tell the yellow bear of Logres something," Scathach said with a merry smile as she popped the head into a leather pouch.

I wanted to go with Scathach's messenger to Avalon, to take Lile's head home. I said I'd won the right. But the old queen wouldn't let me, and the rest agreed, because the journey was too difficult for any but an experienced winter traveler. "And we don't know what Annis or Balin's kin might be up to. Nor what the Lady wants us to do next," they argued. They did agree, though, that the messenger shouldn't take Lile's head. Only a Daughter should perform that duty.

I had the idea Arthur and Nimue would respond by ordering us to find whoever supplied Balin with Lile's head and the steel sword on that night at Camelot. But they didn't. And for their failure, the Celtic Realms bleed on.

For the next month, we stayed prepared for another attack — Scathach would probably have welcomed one — but we also amused ourselves by hunting. The mountain forests teemed with game and Scathach had brought her dogs. Indeed, she seemed to have brought her entire household. The dogs were a strange collection of enormous, sad-eyed hounds and noisy, bearded little terriers.

It wasn't long before Elin was letting half the pack sleep with us. I grew fond of one of the terriers, a scrappy brindle bitch with bright black eyes and a jaunty way of cocking her tail over her back. After long negotiations with Scathach, Elin traded her silver-hilted knife, a brass brooch, and her saddlebags for the little dog.

"Got her cheap," she said with a lying grin when she put the dog in my lap and told me she was mine. The dog — we called her Caitlann — tolerated my delighted hugs and caresses for a breath or two, then jumped down, never to sit on a lap again. Not that Caitlann didn't take to us. She often sat at our feet and would sometimes allow us to scratch her ears. Nor was she bad-tempered. But no matter how often I tried to lure her into my arms, she would have none of it.

All of which Elin found amusing. "The dog's got too good a sense of her own dignity to let you maul her around," she'd say. "If it's canine adoration you want, you should have saved Godgyth from the Grey Ones." Then I'd cry. Godgyth's headless body had been found next to the gate. I made Elin help me bury her according to what she knew of English custom. And I prayed to the English goddess Freyr to protect the poor girl, whoever she'd been before Annis invaded her body, in the dark cold of the English afterworld.

Scathach's message to Arthur apparently had indeed told him something. Her messenger returned just after Imbolc with an invitation from the Pendragon to "All the brave servants of the Mother" to join him in his latest war, this one against the King of Leinster. His excuse for invading Ireland, he said, was to convince "these thick-minded Irish" to stop raiding the British coast. It was a thin excuse, of course. They'd been doing it for generations — Dyvyd was by then more Irish than Welsh. But I suppose Arthur felt he had to keep his warriors happy somehow, now that the English were in flight. "And," he added, with his usual heavy-handed humor, "the Irish are always looking for more dead heroes to sing about."

Elin was delighted by Arthur's letter. She'd been grumbling about having to go back to Calchvynydd. "Pretty dull, this queen business. Let the old men take care of it. I trust them not to cheat me. Besides, I'm a military physician, not a quill-pusher. A soldier. And so are you," she added. "For all the

184

Goddess tried to put you out to permanent pasture. Let's go to Ireland, you and me. It'll be a grand adventure for *British* poets to sing about."

It was tempting, very tempting. Elin and I hadn't yet discussed what we were going to do about the rest of our lives. Her hereditary obligations in Calchvynydd and my Goddess-sworn allegiance to Avalon made the future a tangled thicket indeed. The Irish war would delay any decision indefinitely.

"I suppose Nimue might give me permission," I said as we sat in the now-repaired banqueting hall. "Arthur's letter said she'd already agreed to send half a century."

"Don't even bother with permission, love. As soon as the weather breaks, let's just go. Nimue won't send you to the mines over it. You're her fair-haired girl. Always have been." Elin was feeding Caitlann from the table.

"I've already told her I'd bring back Lile's head."

"Let Faencha or the Hound take it. What does Nimue care, as long as it gets back to Avalon." She teased the dog with a scrap of venison.

Caitlann hoisted herself on her flat rump, into that upright posture those little Scottish dogs know is guaranteed to win over the hardest heart.

"I can't go to Ireland right now, Elin. I've got to wait for Nimue's orders."

Elin tossed the dog the venison.

As it happened, Nimue's instructions arrived the next day. Branwen and the Hound were ordered to Ireland, Branwen to her regular company and the Hound to join a special Gathering that would follow the armies, rescuing war orphans. Faencha and I were to return to Avalon immediately.

I assumed Elin would come to Avalon with me; she assumed I would go to Ireland with her. When it became obvious neither would happen, I simply packed my things, picked up Caitlann, and rode off, leaving Faencha to catch up with me along the way.

As I wound down through the fort's rings, I could hear Elin calling after me. I pulled in my horse and waited for her. Overhead, a flock of geese flew north.

"Don't go," she said, taking my horse's reins. "I want you with me. We could work this out, this mainland-Avalon business. If you wouldn't be so stubborn. Other people have. Meredydd and Briga. Aindrea and Meghan."

"I'm not being stubborn. Nimue wants me to bring Lile home. It's my duty." I glanced at the gilded box strapped to the pack mule behind me.

"What's happened to you? Don't you want any more adventures?"

How could I explain to her? About Godgyth. About Annis. It was going to be hard enough to explain to Nimue. "I've *got* to go to Avalon," I said. "Come with me. We can go to Ireland afterward." The dog squirmed in my arms.

Elin shook her dark head. "I'm not a fool, even if you are. I know what it'll be on Avalon. You'll get stuck there. The Nine'll have you back herding cattle just to prove a point. Can't have people ignoring their calling, you know."

"Nimue —"

"Nimue nothing! She's Lady now and Ladies don't go against the Mother Choice. The only way to get around it is by not going back at all. I knew that the moment I heard Nimue's orders."

"You mean *never* go back?"

"Well —"

"It's my duty."

"Duty, eh?" She grinned. "It's the glory you want. Break out the cider! Bring on the pipers! Argante the Great comes home in triumph!"

"What would *you* know about duty? A queen who forsakes her land. A physician who'd rather kill than heal. Everything has to be the way *you* want it. Well, I'm not like your mother — some hostage who has to please her guard at any price."

Elin's head snapped back, as if I'd struck her. Then her lip curled and she said, "At least my mother could love."

I jerked the reins away from her and shoved Caitlann into her arms, then I kicked my heels into the horse's side.

"You'll regret this, you know!" she yelled after me.

I didn't look back. Then.

Chapter Twelve

Faencha and Meredydd — she'd decided to return to the Island — caught up with me eventually and, as Elin had predicted, we came home in triumph. The games and the feasting lasted for five days and, as Elin had also predicted, I loved it all: loved sitting in one of the chairs of honor with the Nine arrayed at our feet; loved hearing the woman-songs about us; loved the cheering crowds. Of course, it was really Meredydd's triumph and she accepted it with rough good humor until the fourth day when she gathered up Briga and the children to return to

Tref Briga. "Stay and listen to this long enough, you start thinking it's important," she said. "Or that it's going to last."

She was right, of course. The day afterward I was back shoveling cow manure. The Hall herd's. I never did tell Nimue about my — what shall I call it? — my interview with Annis. I decided she'd think I was trying to steal Meredydd's moment. But I did tell her I wanted to go to Ireland.

"Has this sudden interest in foreign wars anything to do with the Queen of Calchvynydd?" she asked, eyebrow raised, the Lady-mark twitching on her cheek.

"Well —"

"There'll be another half-century of Daughters leaving in about a month. They'll need someone to look after their horses. Will that be soon enough?"

I let out a whoop of joy and, against all custom and tradition, caught the tiny Nimue under the arms and swung her off her feet, Lady of the Lake or no. For the next three weeks, I walked around feeling like I'd been chewing on the Healer's mushrooms.

A few days before we were to leave (Faencha was going, too, part of a detachment of Smiths), a Hall-messenger brought me a letter just as the cows were about to be milked. In poor quality army ink, it was addressed simply, "Argante." But I recognized the hand. It was from Elin. Slowly, I ran my finger over the double wolfhound seal of Calchvynydd.

"Eithne," I called to the Chief Herder. "They want me at the Hall. Right now."

From her stool, Eithne gave me a doubting look, which I ignored. She would have doubted a summons from the Mother herself. (As a matter of fact, she did — when I was chosen Lady. But that's another story.) I ran behind the cooling house.

There, leaning against the rock wall, I opened the letter. In her sprawling Latin script, Elin had written: "I received the message about your arrival in Ireland. That won't be necessary. Stay on in Avalon and do your *duty*. You obviously haven't the courage to be any good anywhere else. I want a woman, not a little girl, too scared to find her destiny outside a cowshed." It was unsigned.

I tore up the letter with my teeth, and Faencha went to Ireland without me.

I should have gone, of course. But at first I was plain too angry. Then there was a sudden outbreak of murrain in the Hall herd that frightened the entire Island and kept every Herder and Healer busy until it was quelled. Then a cow stepped on my ankle, still a bit fragile from the injury I'd gotten in Elin's forest, re-breaking it. Then it was winter.

So, almost a year later, when the Hound (with a dozen half-starved babies) came back from the Irish War-gathering, I was still in the City. The second day she was home, she came out to see me in the Lady Line's meadow, where I was repairing a wall.

"Look at her over there," I said, waving in the direction of Epona, our handsomest filly, where she stood pawing the sweet grass. "Ears laid back. Eyes rolling. She's thinking you've come to throw a rope over her. She'll be off over that wall yonder." I shook my fist at the young creature. "And breaking a leg. Then guess who'll have to cut your throat and watch you thrash around till you bleed to death?" As a matter of fact, Epona didn't kill herself on a rock wall. She lived to carry me to my Lady-making, though she did try to dump me at the gate to the Crystal Shrine.

"Life would be a lot simpler without such things," the Hound said as I picked a rock off the pile on the stoneboat. (The break in the wall was serious and I'd had to haul in new stones.)

I wasn't sure whether she meant spirited young animals or rocks, but whichever, for the Hound the statement was high philosophy.

She sat down on the stoneboat to watch as I chipped a corner off the rock then wedged it into place. "Need any help?" Another surprise. The Hound wasn't known for her spirit of cooperation.

"Just getting the tiestones down. They're pretty heavy. How was Ireland? Pretty awful?"

She shrugged and began to tap a stone-chisel against the edge of the boat. "Seen Elin."

"Oh?" I pointed at the long flat rock next to her. "That'll make a good tiestone."

"She's with Faencha."

"Fighting against the King of Leinster. That's hardly news."

We hoisted the rock off the boat. The Hound gazed down at it. "That ain't all they're doing."

The tiestone dropped out of my hands, onto the wall; the wall collapsed at our feet.

For a long time we stared at the rubble. Finally, I said, "I don't think this can be fixed."

And it couldn't, of course. For a while I ignored the sly smirks and pitying looks that followed me in hall and byre, bath and shop and road. No one dared talk of it openly, at least not to me. But I couldn't ignore the stories belted out by every young Poet with a new betrayal to sing about. I began to spend my life in the cheesehouse, stirring the whey, pressing the curd, and churning, churning, churning. I tried to get Claudia to read the Stoic philosophers with me in the evenings. She would have no part of it; said such a thing was unnatural for one of my age.

Finally, I asked to be sent back to Tref Briga.

Nimue received my request — it was a formal one — seated in the council hall, Silver Wheel in its embroidered sheath across her lap and the steel applebranch scepter in her hand. The Nine stood behind her. "But Argante," she said, a puzzled look on her face. "I thought it was Ireland you wanted to go to."

There was a heavy silence and I turned to leave. "Wait, girl!" Fand commanded from her place with the Nine and then whispered into Nimue's ear. She and the Nine withdrew to an outer room. In a few minutes, Nimue returned alone, her expression somewhere between anger and embarrassment.

"Why is the Lady the last to know *anything* on this Island?" She gestured for me to sit on one of the benches. "You didn't go after her. Why? You had several chances."

"I thought I ought to stay — the murrain —"

"Ought." She shook her head. "Ought. And this is a formal request, so I *ought* to be holding branch and sword." She picked up Silver Wheel and the steel branch and held them stiff-armed in front of her. They were heavy things, and the sword almost as tall as Nimue herself. She held them that way for a long time, until I could see her arms begin to shake with fatigue and the black Lady-mark on her cheek grow grey. At last, she let sword and branch drop. The clatter filled the hall.

She left them where they lay and came and knelt down in front of me. "Foolish, foolish girl." She put her arms around me.

After we cried for a while, she asked, "What is it you want to do now?"

"Die," I said.

The weather has continued to be dry, though the coughing-sickness has abated some. The Healers tell me it will probably reassert itself in the spring; winter has only slowed it a bit. Winter has certainly slowed me. My hands have been too sore with chilblain to write, though I sit in the baths half the day.

I've never cared for the chatter of company in the baths. Perhaps because in my childhood the command *Silence,* written in more than one place on the marble walls, was sternly and vigorously enforced. Or at least I think it was. At any rate, I prefer to lie like an old moss-covered rock as the hot, healing water is poured down over me. The cooling-room is the place for talk, when your spirit is as relaxed as your muscles.

It's there I like to listen to the women sing, even if the songs are sad, as they generally are these days. Last week, Flann and Macha sang one called "Man of Logres, Man of Blood." It had a haunting kind of melody in the old style and the words were well-chosen, if plain. But I asked them to spare me of it in the future. It's about Arthur's Irish war.

For two years I hid in Tref Briga, never going to the City and rarely hearing its news, except for the occasional scrap: that a storm had smashed some of the Hall's glass panels, that Boann Bignose was with child again, that Nimue had been ill, that the Lady Lyonesse had come calling. We also heard that Arthur's Irish war had become a debacle and Nimue had recalled the Daughters — but not soon enough. Already twenty or thirty had been killed. Including Faencha, that splendid girl, dead on the green plain of Kildare.

I wept when I heard, of course, and cursed and rent my clothes. But all the time I thought how Elin will come back to me. She didn't.

That autumn, I decided to go to the City for Samain. It's not my favorite festival — too much magic and too many cattle — but I wanted to see Claudia. Nessa had died the previous winter and I didn't think Claudia would be interested in life without her. Something I was finding that I could understand.

Meredydd was going to get a new saddle and Aline hoped she might swap her year's worth of cowhides for a book, so we packed the mules with trade goods and left Tref Briga in the hands of old Longshank and Olwen, who never went to the City. Olwen did, though, send along the English head she kept on the post by her front door. For luck, she said. Briga brought her youngest set of twins, now three years old. She had had no more children.

We also had half a dozen cows with us, one to sacrifice and the others as Lady tribute. As a result, the trip took considerably longer than it would otherwise. And we were slowed by the Island custom of consuming the last of the previous year's cider along the way. Each pack mule bore two huge barrels. Of course, by Samain some of the cider is more vinegar than anything, but the rest is guaranteed to make a very merry trip indeed.

About noon of the last day, when we were almost in sight of the City, we stopped in the Near Hills to let the cows graze and chew their cuds. The Hills, just beginning to turn brown, stood in crisp relief against the sun, their outcroppings of sandy limestone glistening. We could hear the noise of the competitions and began to make bets on who would be the first to see the pennons atop the Lady Hall. Meredydd had won the last two years, but, as I loudly reminded everyone, this year, I of the extraordinary eyesight was along.

"The cider you've put away, I doubt you're able to see past your horse's ears," Briga commented as she stood swaying beside her piebald old he-mule.

"Quite so," Aline added. "Your wonderful eyesight has not allowed you to notice that Augusta Bovina has wandered up the valley."

Aline had a way of talking that set my teeth on edge.

But, sure enough, Augusta Bovina, dun-colored and mean-tempered, was ambling toward a patch of tansy. I whistled one of the dogs after her, but his pursuit only set her running. It's just that sort of thing that makes cattle such an aggravation. Most of them are dumb and docile, but the odd one is the Hag's own creature. I chased her the rest of the day, over hills, through woods and bogs. Now and then she'd stop and stare back at me with those vacant brown eyes, then tear off again. And, frankly, the cider I'd been working on for three days didn't help, either. I only sobered up after my horse slipped in a streambed and I took a good cold soaking.

So I missed the opening of Samain, when the Lady goes down into the underground temple with the Sacred Bull and the Nine heap dirt around its door, then sacrifice seven white oxen. At dawn she emerges (Lug, the Bull, is always slow about knocking the door open, lazy wretch that he is) and declares that the night is joined to the day, the old year to the new, the Mother to the Realms. Then the feast called One Together begins.

This Samain had drawn a big crowd from the mainlands. Morgant was there, as usual, to show off by flying the Crystal Shrine's quartzstone boulder around the bay a few times. She was a great one for levitating rocks. I can't think why. My other aunt, Margawse, and her daughter, my cousin Clarisant, had come, too, Margawse leaning heavily on her son Medraut's arm. She was still in mourning, she said, for Lot, who had died in the Irish war. And Gwenhyfar was in the City because "Samain is so dull these days at Camelot without dear Arthur." She had handsome young Perceval Dragon Butcher in tow, though I think Perceval would have preferred masculine company.

"Dear Arthur" was not present because he was still in Ireland, of course. Morgant and Nimue were, it was said, working to effect an alliance between the Pendragon and MacErca, king of Ailech in northern Ireland. MacErca's army would clean up the mess in Leinster, in return for which he would be made High King of Ireland. And Arthur could escape with what remained of his honor — and his army.

Nor was this the first time Morgant the Merlin Falcon had gone about pulling Arthur's parsnips out of the fire. It was Morgant who had planned the early battles against the English, and Morgant who had called down the lightning when Arthur was trapped on Badon. Morgant had rebuilt the temple to the sun-god on Salisbury Plain. Morgant had saved the King from the red dragon in the forest of Dean. And had salted its tail and made it and all its kind bow down before the King of Logres. Morgant it was who had smoothed over Arthur's various beddings of other men's wives (once even yanking him out of Margawse's window as Lot himself stove in the door).

But Ireland was to be the last time Morgant came to Arthur's aid. On the second day of Samain, while I was watching Augusta Bovina chew her cud — she was by then securely tied to the end of a rope — Nimue abdicated. Then she and Morgant, two white seabirds, flew away.

All sorts of wild stories have been told about the whole business. As a matter of fact, only a few days ago I heard Deirdre trying to tell Flann and Macha that Nimue had cast Morgant into a crystal cave.

"Preposterous!" I shouted at her from my chair by the fire. She cringed a bit and shuffled out. To empty the chamberpot, she said.

"Good job for her," the tall one, Flann,

commented when Deirdre'd gone. "Lady, what *did* happen with Morgant then? They also say she was still suffering from some kind of madness. It'd made her run naked through a forest in Scotland."

Now, I'd always thought Morgant a bit mad, but the only person I've ever heard to run naked through a forest was Kai and that had to do with some kind of punishment Christians inflict on themselves. I told Flann that as far as I was concerned what really happened that Samain was far worse than any mainland gleeman's lies.

It happened this way:

After the One Together feast, Nimue, with Morgant, led the crowd out to the Crystal Shrine. There, still in her red Lady-robe, she kissed the applebranch scepter and Silver Wheel, then took them inside the Shrine. When she came out, she was empty-handed. "The branch and the sword belong once again to the Mother alone. My hands can no longer hold them."

The crowd gasped. "I can no longer place Avalon above all else, as I promised to do at my Lady-making. I — we —" She stuttered into silence.

Morgant gently took her arm and said, more to her than the crowd, "Our lives must be our own. Not Avalon's. Not Arthur's."

And with no more than that, they changed themselves into seabirds and soared out over the bay, leaving everyone staring open-mouthed after them.

The two birds swooped and dove and frolicked in the joy of their flight until they were two tiny dots just above the horizon. Two dots. Then three, then twelve, then a whole sky of dark forms, sweeping back toward the Island. And with them came a grey mist. It turned the water from azure to slate, then hid it altogether. Soon it was a great cloud of fog, covering the City and fields and creeping up into the hills. Finally, it engulfed the Lady Hall; not even the flag of Avalon thrust up above it.

Then the crowd heard the filthy cries of starlings and when the fog lifted, the Island was in the hands of the Grey Host. And Annis.

Of course, I knew nothing of all this as I pulled, and sometimes pushed, Augusta Bovina through the long flat valley toward the City. So poky was she that I finally dismounted and walked behind her to give her a good swat with a thorn stick when she tried my patience beyond endurance. Her response was to quick-step a couple of yards, glance back at me with her stupid brown stare, blow a few bubbles of green cud, and slow down again.

At mid-afternoon, as we wound along the base of a steep hill, the bare trees on the ridge opposite became a black tangle against a pale, white sun. Fog began to roll up the valley. For a moment, the animals shivered nervously. Then they bolted.

Twenty yards away, a troop of Grey Ones emerged from the fog. The sick-sweet stench of death clung to them.

There were perhaps a dozen, only lightly armed with spears and swords, and without shields. I, on the other hand, was not armed at all, except for a knife and my sling. I grabbed for the sling, but, in my cider-muddled state, I hadn't wound it correctly and it caught in my belt. As I tore at it, a Grey

One streaked forward to hurl his spear, then follow it with his body in one of those suicidal attacks the Host call military tactics.

It was something I could handle, even with only a knife. I thrust the knife forward and let the weight of his great pale body do the work. He went down, pus-colored blood pouring from his belly. There was no doubt he was dead, but his fall had jerked the knife from my hand. I looked up to see the rest of the Grey Ones rushing at me, spears lowered for the kill. Their spittle sprayed in the air.

I turned and started a mad scramble up the steep hillside. One spear, two, shot past to bury themselves in the grass beside me. The steep incline was cluttered with rocks and stone outcroppings, which I alternately slipped on and clung to. Somehow, I managed to pull out of spear range, but the climb took my breath quickly. From terror, I suppose. I knew I could not go far.

The wooded hilltop was a hundred yards up. But just below the crest I spotted a small lightning-struck oak, fallen across a ditch. The tree's leaves still clung to it and their tangle formed a barricade. I headed for it, Grey Ones following. They were clumsy and slow and I succeeded in reaching the tree. The ditch, more a depression in the brown grass really, was crammed with wet leaves and I had to shovel them away with my hands to get good footing.

Through the branches, I had a good view of the slope and saw fog rolling up from the valley. Annis's handiwork, I had no doubt.

In climbing the hill, the Grey Ones had had to break their close formation. Now, two were using small cedar trees for cover as they moved up on my left. On my right, another scuttled between some flat-topped boulders. The rest continued up slowly, taking the same route I had.

My hands shook but I was at last able to unscramble the sling and get a stone out of my stone-pouch. I stepped out of the cover of branches, took aim, fired at the Grey One among the rocks. He went down and stayed down. But by then the two on the left were almost close enough to use their spears. I broke cover again, hurling the stone quickly before I dived back behind the branches. It caught the Grey One in the act of throwing and the spear fell wide, among the oak branches. I snatched it up, to add to my tiny arsenal.

Spearless now, the Grey One unsheathed his sword and he and his companion moved in. I had the presence of mind to step out and throw the spear just as the first one got close. It pierced his light armor and he fell dead. The others, though, were almost on me.

Slings aren't much good at close range. So, to get some distance, I made for a little clearing at the crest of the hill. There, I shoved a stone in the sling's cradle and swung it over my head, aiming at the first Grey One I saw. A hand around my wrist stopped me. Then something snapped my arms back and pinned them behind me.

"Argante . . ." a voice called from a long way off. "Argante . . ." I twisted around. A Grey One held me.

"Argante . . ." I turned my head. No one was there. Even the Grey Ones on the slope had disappeared.

"Argante . . . Argante . . . Argante . . ." The bell-like sound reverberated through the fog from invisible hill to invisible hill. In the air there hung the smell of burnt cloves.

Chapter Thirteen

The Grey One unloosed me and moved back, but I remained frozen. The voice came nearer and the scent of burnt cloves grew stronger, mixed now with the smell of my own fear.

She stepped out of the fog in a swirl of mist and white cloak, her eyes the blue of a distant mountain. The rings on her fingers gleamed darkly as she brushed back a strand of pale gold hair.

I dove for the sling lying a few feet away. But before I could reach it, her foot fell on my arm. The

Grey One seized me and pulled me up. I gagged at the reek of him.

"There'll be no playing with slings this time," Annis said, with her laugh like a bell. Then she swept out her hand and the fog dropped away. Below lay the valley, rich with grass and plantain and tansy and gentian. Through it wound a stream, brown and sluggish here, there white and glittering as it broke over rock. In a little patch of sandy bank, my horse was rolling, satisfying some itch in his sleek black hide. Augusta Bovina stood not far off, the grass as tall as her chest.

The fog returned and Annis waved off the Grey One that held me. She put her hand on my shoulder. "Avalon is beautiful, is it not?"

"Are you going to kill me?"

"Shall we claim it, you and I? This sweet island? With Nimue gone now—"

I glanced from Annis to the Grey One to the woods. I wondered if I could reach the woods before the Grey One's spear reached me.

"Gone off with Morgant. Thrown down the branch and the sword. Stripped off her duty as lady as if it were a dirty garment."

"Morgant?"

"Come, let's fly away to the City and see what you'll have when *you're* Lady."

"Lady?"

Her fingernails dug into my shoulder and she yanked me around so that her face was close to mine. "Don't play the idiot-girl with me, Pendragondaughter," she hissed. "You may have fooled Avalon with your clowning, but I know you for what you are. And *you* know what I'm saying.

You have your father's — Well, he's never had ambition so much as . . . illusion. He can rule the world, but he needs help. From his kin. And without his dear little sister, Morgant, *you* will have to supply his help."

She threw out her hand and I saw Cadwallon the Slug's dead body caught in the reeds of the lake. On the shore stood Medraut, my half-brother. Then Annis showed me Medraut snatching up Lile's severed head on that awful night at Camelot.

She released my arm and smiled. "So let's fly — But, of course, you can't fly. You have no magic. No center. I'll have to bring the City to you."

Again, she swept out her elegantly ringed hand. The fog rose, then fell away. Where the valley had been, there was now the City. The Grey Host had it cordoned off: the gates, the wall, the quay bristled with the instruments of war. The people, those who had come for Samain, had been stripped of weapons and divided into small groups, guarded at sword-point by Grey Ones. They must not have surrendered too easily, for there were bodies lying in the streets.

Annis somehow maneuvered the vision so that I could not identify most of the people. But among a group of prisoners on the Parade Ground, I did see Briga and Meredydd. They sat in the lank, desolate slump of defeat. Beside them, their children played with the black head of Olwen's Englishman.

Up at the Hall, Gwenhyfar and Perceval, too, were prisoners, but of a different sort. They sat with Claudia in her quarters, Perceval and Claudia calmly playing chess while Gwenhyfar, a cider barrel close by her, rattled on about their predicament.

Annis next produced the Council-hall. It crawled with Grey Ones, some rolling barrels, others toting goods; some bearing reports, others receiving orders. And here Medraut was ensconced. When I saw him, it was clear who was in command on Avalon. He lounged in the Lady-chair, one leg thrown over its bronze arm. Annis showed him to me close-up and I could see the pleasure in his cloudy grey eyes as he alternately barked orders and fingered the goods the Grey Ones brought him — linen and wool, leather and steel, gold and fur — all that made up the material wealth of Avalon. "Medraut's little reward," Annis explained. "For bagging Lile's head and the Great Sword that night at Camelot."

Margawse and Clarisant, his mother and sister, were with him. At a table near the wall, Clarisant sat interrogating Fedelm, the Chief Healer, an old woman somewhat hard of hearing, about the location of the healing herbs. "I will know where they are or you'll be dead by nightfall!"

Fedelm pulled at a strand of white forelock and looked more puzzled than frightened by the sharp words. "Nightshade? Try any wall. But it'll kill you, you know."

Clarisant ordered her away.

The rest of the Nine were nowhere to be seen. I learned later that Clarisant had had them bound and thrown in the privy.

Margawse stood behind Medraut, countermanding half his orders so that the Grey Ones trying to carry them out would get to one door only to be called back and sent off through another. The Council-hall looked like an anthill some child had stirred into hysteria.

"Such is the condition of Avalon," Annis said. The City disappeared into fog. "The people need a Lady. And they need her now."

The chaos in the City was appalling, but I knew, and I said, "They wouldn't want *me.*"

"They'd fall down on their faces at your feet, if I bade them."

In my mind, I saw myself at the Crystal Shrine, the Sacred Bull by my side. Kneeling before me were the Nine. Already Fand, Eithne, the Hound had kissed my breast in submission and supplication to me as Lady of the Lake.

It was ludicrous. I laughed.

Annis caught me by the neck of my tunic and slapped me. "Perhaps you won't deny *everything* you love." Her eyes were the color of a dark sea now. She flung out her hand. The fog rose, fell. "Look," she said.

Below, a battle raged. In it I saw Arthur and Lancelot and Bedwyr. They were hacking their way through wave after wave of mailed Irish. I could hear the snap of bones and the shrieks of men and horses as they died. Elin was amongst them. But she was down, shield and Healer's bag both gone, sword-arm limp. An Irishman stood over her, sword raised to strike the deathblow.

I screamed.

The Irishman's sword stopped in mid-stroke. He went statue-still. Everywhere the battle did the same. Horses stopped in stride. Battleshouts froze in throats. Spears paused in the air. The dying hovered between life and death. Then the fog fell over them.

Annis laid her hand on my shoulder once more. "You want this girl to live."

"I —"

"If you do, let us — you and I — pick up the sword and the branch."

It was too much. I grabbed her by the throat and wrenched her to the ground. "You will not harm Elin!" I yelled it into her face and gouged my thumb into her eye. The eye popped out of its socket.

She threw me off easily, batted me away as she would an annoying insect. I'd caught her by surprise, but when I looked up from where we'd fallen, there were Grey Ones all around me, swords drawn. In the distance, I heard the low rumble of thunder.

Annis stood. She drew up a corner of white cloak and pressed it to her eye. "If you've made me ugly —" She succeeded in pushing the eye back into its socket, but it seemed askew and her brow and mouth were puckered in pain. "You have your father's arrogance, I see. And his brutality." She dabbed the cloak at her seeping eye. "A good thing, in fact." She ordered the Grey Ones back. "Together, the three of us can —"

Another drumbeat of thunder interrupted her. It was closer this time. The snow began to fall, hard pellets mixed with cold rain.

Annis snapped her head up. Her eyes slewed around in search of — what? I wondered. "So, you're interfering with me again," she snarled. "Where are you, you bitch?"

Another thunderclap filled the air.

Where they stood, encircling me, the Grey Ones began to dissolve. First their weapons melted away, then their heads collapsed like rotten pumpkins and slid down over their shoulders. In a matter of a few breaths, all that remained of them were stinking puddles of yellow slime.

Annis ran through the clearing first one way, then the other, all the time screeching out curses in the old language. I stayed where I lay, rooted, terrified.

Lightning bolts began to strike the small trees that dotted the hill's slope. They burst into flame, one after another. It was like an army moving up the hill. I rolled myself up into a small ball, hiding my head, shielding my ears from the noise.

Then, except for the soft hiss of the rainy snow against the ground, there was silence.

"Here I am, sister." The voice was soft, musical.

I peeked over my arms. Annis had stopped. She stared past me. I looked back.

At the edge of the woods stood Augusta Bovina. "I think it's time you went home, sister," she said, waddling toward Annis.

The beast smelled of fresh flowers and springtime and even I knew that this was the Goddess, come to us as a cow.

"Please, Mother," I found the courage to whisper, reaching out to touch her leg as she passed. "Elin?"

"Alive, well." She did not take her eyes off Annis.

Annis's shoulders slumped. But she quickly drew herself up and pulled the cloak over her damaged eye. "I can dry up oceans, crumble mountains," she said in a loud, determined voice. "Stop the rain, silence the springs, freeze the sun. I can even send the snakes crawling back to Ireland."

"I know you can, dear. But not just now." The Mother twitched her muddy right ear.

Annis raised her hand to call up the fog. Nothing happened. She swept her hand out again, wider this time, angrier. Still no fog rose. The snow continued in big, soft flakes now.

"This is not the place for you, sister. Gather up your . . . things and leave us," the Mother said. Her tail switched up over her back.

Annis glanced at her for another moment, then, in the brief space of a bat of an eyelash, she was gone.

I still huddled on the wet ground, unable to summon even the courage to look around to see if perhaps Annis was perched on an oak branch behind me.

"Stand up, Argante," the Mother said. And I did, slowly, with great reluctance.

"Who are you?" she asked, facing me now, her brown eyes no longer blankly bovine. They gave out a warm glow that calmed my terror enough for me to answer.

"Argante . . . Herder from Tref Briga."

"And?"

I tried again. "Gwenhyfar's child? Arthur's? . . . Lancelot's?"

"I see you, like Annis, mistake blood for flesh." A ripple ran over her hide, still thick with its winter hair.

I heard the crash of the thunder, saw the trees and sky turn white before I felt the lightning bolt smash through me. The next thing I knew, I was once again in the mud, paralyzed and believing every bone in my body had been shattered. The metal torque burned against my neck and there was a searing pain in my left cheekbone. Snow still fell.

"You are Argante, Lady of the Lake," the Mother said. "Touch your cheek and you will find the Lady-mark, clean, black, fresh."

Slowly, I raised my hand to my still-tingling face. With my fingertips I traced the oval and the crescent that topped it.

"Now go and take up the sword and the branch."

I struggled to my feet, aching all over. I could barely speak. My throat had closed down and my tongue clove to the roof of my mouth. I had spent my life among cattle. What could I know about rule, about the duties of the Mother's bondswomen? "Why —?"

"That is a question you will be a lifetime answering."

"But I have no magic. I think that's why Annis —" I stopped, waiting for her to explain or at least to tell me how to be Lady. "There must be sacred words I should know. Like the Healers say over their herbs."

"Nor mistake mystery for flesh. You have all the magic you will ever need."

And that is the last thing the Mother ever said to me. From that day to this, I was on my own.

As I stood gaping at her, the snow stopped and the sweet green smell of spring faded from her. It was replaced by a barnyard stench of manure and wet straw. The cow was once again Augusta Bovina, ugly, mean-tempered, and just then trotting off into the woods, her rope trailing through the mud.

I picked up my sling and followed.

* * * * *

And that is the story I wanted to tell when I ordered Deirdre to bring me ink and hide and cider. And that is the story I labored to put down all the cold, dry winter. But now it is summer again. And I have another story to tell:

The ceremonies and games of my Lady-making took up most of the first summer of my reign, two years ago. Once again the mighty of the Celtic realms descended on Avalon. All the mighty except Arthur. He sent seven shiploads of tribute and his regrets. Nor did Elin come. Or any of the Daughters who had gone to Ireland. The war raged on.

It was not until the next spring that our troops returned. Some of them, anyway. I welcomed those few back on a day so hot I could hardly distinguish the sweat that poured down my face from my tears. Once again, Elin had not come to Avalon.

Meanwhile, the rains stopped.

And Fand died. She'd done her job as Chief Child Gatherer well, so well that during her tenure Avalon's population had doubled and doubled again. Sadly, in the process, she abused her body and ended her days a toothless old crone, able only to sit by the fire while her womb-daughters fed her gruel. She died in the early spring, just before the Year Gathering set out for the mainlands.

"I'm damned if I'll watch another one go without me," she said as I sat by what turned out to be her deathbed.

"Oh, Fand," I lied, "you'll be able to go this year. I'll see to it, if they have to take you on a litter. There's not one of them who's got any kind of nose for tracking. Not even the Hound." I grinned. "And yours is cold and wet still."

The old woman squinted up at me. "Lady you may be, Argante. But you're just as silly as you ever were."

She died the next morning.

Then, in this, the third summer of my reign, Branwen rode into the Hall yard. The noise of the geese and the dogs brought me up out of the byre where I was inspecting the Hall herd. (Being Lady has not freed me from cattle.) When I saw who it was, I wrenched her off her horse, screeching louder than geese and dogs together. She'd returned from Ireland bone-thin and with her skin, usually a warm cream, now yellow and blotched. She looked worn out. Except for her eyes. They were a blue blaze.

I thought it odd that she hadn't come immediately to the Crystal City but instead had disembarked in the north. But she said she'd been anxious to visit her womb-mother in Tref Arainrhod.

Seonaid laid on a supper fit for a visiting goddess: both veal and lamb, pickled eggs and pigsfeet still dripping with brine, great bowls of stewed parsnips, watercress, loaf after loaf of bread, and a mountain of butter to spread on it or yogurt flavored with dill to dip it in. All served with the last of the good Spanish wine and followed by nuts and dried Island apples.

But Branwen ate little of it. Instead, she talked about the war. Indeed, she could not seem to stop talking of it. Of the blood and noise and filth of the battlefields, of Arthur's slaughter of his hostages, of the hunger of his troops. Trapped with few provisions on alien soil, they'd eaten their bridles and drunk the mud in the horses' tracks until they devoured the horses themselves. "Then we ate the bark off the trees."

"How come you didn't get back with the rest of the Daughters when the King of Leinster let them pass through his lines?" The Hound, now one of the Nine, asked the question, slopping more wine into her cup.

Branwen said, "I stayed on with Elin and Faencha." She stood up. "It took Faencha a long time to die."

Thanking me for the hospitality of the Hall, she picked up her bedroll and went outside. Walls, she said, made her nervous now.

The next day Seonaid suggested we have fish for supper. Wanting to talk to Branwen alone, I volunteered to go catch some. But we had little luck. By the end of the day we'd only gotten three rather smallish pike. "Nasty looking brutes," I said as I held them up for Branwen to see.

"You asked about Faencha a while ago," she said, facing across the mountain lake toward the little Mother shrine that sat on its far bank. "On the plains of Kildare, it was. The fighting had gone on all day. In the rain and fog. She took a spear to the stomach. We got her away, but it wouldn't heal. One of Arthur's poets made a song about her, naturally. As if that'll give her immortality." She still faced the lake.

"'Woman of bright glory,' it goes. 'Who laughed in battle, who slew, who burned from dawn to dawn. She longed for war, made food for dark-beaked

214

hawks. She deserves praise and sweet mead.' Ridiculous, isn't it?"

I put the pike on the ground and squatted down to clean them. They lay on the grass like three soldiers flopped down after a losing battle, exhausted but still armed, dangerous if given the opportunity. I said that, personally, I rather liked the song and thought Faencha would have, too.

Branwen glanced briefly at me. "But she died in the arms of her lord."

Faencha with a man? What about Elin? I grabbed a fish around its slick green belly and slid the blade of my knife behind a gill.

As I turned the knife and pressed down to cut the head off, Branwen said, "The Lord Jesus Christ. Faencha was a Christian. So am I. So is Elin."

The knife crunched through the backbone and the head came off. Fish guts spilled over my hands. The pike's body fluttered and its mouth still struck at an unseen enemy.

"We were converted by Brigid in Kildare. She's a good woman —"

Brigid! Who took the things of the Mother! Who'd stolen the sacred fire at Kildare, murdered its priestess, set up her own foul establishment instead. What did they call it? A monastery? Anyway, a hall where Christians went to hide from the world.

"Ah, Brigid," I said, without looking up. "Isn't she the one who goes around saying she turned a lake into beer? Some story. Though I once heard that the Mother —"

"There is but one god, Argante. What you call the Mother is only Satan's handmaiden."

Then Branwen began to run on about the man

215

she called the Christ and his life and assorted miracles. She sounded like the half-wit girl some seducing villain has told she's beautiful. I finished cleaning the fish in silence.

Finally, I said, "Enough! I won't hear any more about your life-hating, woman-hating, foreign god." I packed the fish into a sack and whistled for my horse. "Where's Elin now?"

"In Ireland. She's a nun at Brigid's monastery," Branwen answered. "The Irish call her a saint."

Chapter Fourteen

I didn't believe it.

And neither did the Hound. "Let me beat the truth out of her," she said the next evening as we sat in the Lady Garden. The setting sun splashed copper across the bay.

The thought of the skinny little Hound flailing away at Branwen, taller even than I and much heavier, made me laugh out loud. "I think Sister Branwen would welcome the opportunity to be a martyr for the Christian god," I replied. "For some people there are worse punishments than being whipped."

The Hound snorted her disbelief. She still looked tired, but no longer coughed, I was glad to note.

"Besides, you know Branwen is just about impervious to pain." We both remembered the time Branwen's horse fell on her up in the High Pasture and she'd walked all the way to the House of Healing with the bone sticking out of her shin like a divining rod.

"Starve her, then. She sure ain't imper . . . imper . . . she sure likes her food," the Hound pointed out. Branwen was always first in line for every meal and last to leave the table. "But I suppose that'd be martyrdom, too. Och, these Christians are mad. Too bad we can't stick 'em all in a seacave like we got Branwen. That'd teach 'em."

"That's it, Hound!" I said and threw my arms around her. "*You* should be called Argante instead of me. *You're* the brilliant one!" I left the Hound digging her hand into her black hair, looking puzzled.

That night I had Branwen relieved of Christian books and artifacts. Then I sent her a message informing her that since she was an Island-born servant of the Mother, I had no intention of letting her return to Ireland. She could, however, leave the cave anytime she wanted and come to the Hall, where she would be provided for in every way and even employed should she grow bored.

That was a mistake. When Branwen took up residence in the Hall, she spent day and night praying. At the top of her voice. Finally, I could stand it no longer. She went back to the cave.

After a month and a half, though, Branwen surrendered at last. She agreed to tell me what she knew of Elin's whereabouts, in return for which I would send her back to her Irish monastery.

"It's a trick," Eithne said in council that night. I'd put the Chief Herder as far away from me as possible in the Circle of the Nine, but the smell of cowshit still permeated the room. I reminded myself to have it re-done in cedar, forgetting the cedar had burned with the rest of the Island's trees.

"Branwen's had time to invent tall tales aplenty," Eithne continued, sucking at a strand of her dirty read hair. "Face it, girl — Lady, I mean. Elin's dead. Gone with Arawn and his dogs to the Otherworld. We should be considering how we're going to feed the Island now you've slaughtered the cattle." She sneered. "But, of course, kept the pigs."

For a moment I wanted to ram Silver Wheel down her throat and out her big rump. Instead, I laid the sword and branch across my lap and sent for Branwen.

"Sit down," I said when she entered, waving at the blue tweed pillow in the middle of the circle.

"I prefer to stand," she said. Her voice was low and controlled, but she ran a hand through her curls. I recognized the gesture as the only indication of nervousness she ever gave.

"I don't know why you've turned against the Mother," I began.

Eithne interrupted me. "It don't take much to figure that out. She thought she was going to be Lady. Sure, we all did. And when the Mother chose like she done, Branwen turned vengeful." Eithne hawked and spat, as if the Hall's polished floor were the dirt of any cowshed. "All them Sheepherder's from up Tref Arianrhod's like that. Don't get their way, they burn your barn."

I ignored Eithne, though she was right about Tref Arianrhod. "Where is Elin?" I asked. "I know she's no nun." Nor saint, either.

"Swear you'll send me back to Brigid."

Back to Brigid? Not back to Jesus? Well, well, I thought. "I will, by the Mother."

Branwen and I looked at each other for a long while in silence. We had spent nearly a lifetime together and though she had rejected the Mother as she would a thorn in her finger, I did not believe she could so easily shed the skin of Avalon. She would tell me the truth.

The Nine began to shift their chairs and clear their throats. Branwen glanced at them rather disdainfully, then returned her gaze to me and said, "For all I know, your Elin is dead. I must tell you that straightaway."

"But you don't think so."

She shook her head.

"Then tell me what happened in Ireland."

The night after Faencha's wake ended, Branwen said, some of Arthur's men staggered out of the monastery's woodlot, bloody and pale with exhaustion. The gatekeeper stopped them at the outer wall and they begged sanctuary. There were three of them, an extraordinarily tall man and two shorter ones. They were unarmed, bearing only their Dragon Shields. One of the shorter men, a greasy-haired blond with milky grey eyes, did the talking. He explained they were the remnants of the Pendragon's rear guard and had been cut off from their army, now in full flight. He also asked if it was true that an Avalon-trained physician was in residence, as they had heard from the local peasantry. The gatekeeper, a monk from the west who had little use for the King of Leinster and his wars, bade them enter. The blond man leaned heavily on the giant.

When the gatekeeper saw the extent of their wounds, he immediately took them to the round rock hut occupied by Elin and Branwen, where he left them.

Once inside, the three wasted no time. The two shorter men grabbed the sleeping women by the hair, looped ropes around their necks, and pulled tight. Meanwhile, the giant drew a sword from beneath his cloak, and with it dispatched the snarling, biting Caitlann. The little dog died with her teeth sunk in his ankle.

Branwen woke in terror. As she struggled against the rope, the man above her pushed her down and pulled the noose so tight she began to choke. "Stay put," he said. "And you won't get hurt." He eased the tension on the rope a bit and Branwen could breathe again.

In the shadows on the other side of the hut's single room, the blond man spoke to Elin in a low, nearly muffled voice. "You will come with us."

Elin made no response.

"As you wish," he said and there was a crunching sound followed by a strangled moan.

Dark though the hut was, Branwen saw the man haul Elin's unconscious body out of the bed. He lowered her to the floor and stripped off the wool Calchvynydd tartan cloak she slept in. Beneath it,

221

was naked. The man then took off his own cloak and trousers and beckoned the giant to help him get Elin into them.

The giant nudged Elin with his bleeding foot and asked something in a guttural language Branwen didn't know but thought might be English. She didn't like the tone of his voice.

"Later," the blond man said in Celtic.

"Huh?" the giant grunted. When the other man spoke a word or two in the guttural language, the giant nodded and laughed.

After the fair-haired man had exchanged clothes with Elin, he turned to Branwen. "Stay here and make no sound or this monastery will be in flames before morning and you and every living thing in it will be dead," he said in Celtic. The words were muffled but menacing. Then he motioned to the giant, who hoisted Elin into his arms and left the hut. The man holding Branwen dropped the rope and followed.

In the doorway, the blond man paused for a moment to kick aside the dog's body.

It was a moonlit night and Branwen recognized him.

She tugged the rope away from her throat. "Where are you taking her, Medraut?"

Medraut walked over to the bed and, leaning so close Branwen could see his milky grey eyes and smell his hair like rancid bacon, he said, "If you tell anyone who you saw here tonight, I will not only burn this place, I will see to it that Brigid and all her nuns feel the iron of English pricks in cunt and ass and eye."

With that, he, too, left.

"And no one stopped them?" I asked when Branwen had finished.

"They told the gatekeeper that the Healer would tend to the wounded man at their camp, where there were other wounded soldiers."

I looked around the circle at the Nine. Except for Eithne, who appeared disbelieving, and old Fedelm, who was asleep, their faces were closed. I turned back to Branwen. "Do you swear this by your god?"

She folded her hands and held them to her breast. "I swear it by God the Father, God the Son, and God the Holy Ghost."

Just who all these gods were, I wasn't sure. But they sounded like a most powerful triad and I believed her. A carragh left for Ireland on the next tide.

After I'd dismissed Branwen and the rest of the Nine had gone from the Council-hall, the Hound wondered why Branwen had come to Avalon with her wild tale about Elin having turned Christian. I said I wondered myself and wished Claudia well enough to help me figure it out. "What's important, though," I commented after we'd shaken our heads in bewilderment for a while, "what's important is that we know where Elin is."

"We do?"

"In a village in Suth Seaxe. And we're going after her."

When I told the Nine what I intended to do, they, of course, had their usual tantrum. "Hissies," Claudia always called these episodes of collective displeasure. "They hiss and spit and caterwaul like so many scalded tabbies. What they need is the cold water of a little reason."

And it was a little reason I tried to give them. "I know, I know. Medraut is trying to lure me away from Avalon," I told them. "I know he wants to isolate me. I know Annis is behind all this. I know. I know. But . . ."

But the hissy boiled on until I finally sent them away and informed Flann and the Hound we would be leaving for the British mainland at the new moon. I had already sent Macha to Tref Briga with orders that Meredydd should gather up troops to go with us to the mainland.

Meanwhile, I contrived to let the Nine believe that their hissy had put out the fire of my passion to rescue Elin. Contritely, I told them that I would soon go to inspect the northern garrisons. Word had come that morale was extremely low up there, what with the heat and reduced rations. And perhaps I should have gone. Lile surely would have. But I knew that my presence would only be a palliative; I could not cure the drought. I could, however, find Elin.

At the new moon, we set out looking like the Lady of the Lake and her retinue: I clothed in scarlet and seated in Epona's high gilt saddle, the Hound in her green Gatherer's garments and carrying the sword and branch, Flann going before flying the blue standard of Avalon. Deirdre would dearly have loved to go along, but I bought her off by leaving her in charge of the Lady Hall, the Crystal City, and, indeed, the whole Island. How the Nine loved that!

Nightfall found our little parade conveniently close to the eastern shore, where Meredydd and Macha had carraghs waiting. My description of the

kind of troops I would require had been explicit, and
Meredydd had provided a dozen of them. She looked
sad as she stood with the horses on the shingle
where we cast anchor, like a little girl who can't go
out and play. But Briga had made her promise she
would stay on Avalon to fight the drought with the
rest of their clan.

Nor did we take pouches filled with dirt. There
would be no shape-shifting this time. No Island birds
would fly from this danger.

The carraghs were old and not especially sound
— I wanted it to look as if we were Islanders
escaping the troubles — and the Hound, though an
excellent sailor as all Gatherers must be, found she
had her work cut out to safely navigate the long
way to the British mainland. However, with fair
winds, sent by the Mother herself I didn't doubt, we
put ashore in a little less than a week, tired,
sunburnt, but whole.

And before long we had reached the oak-forested
hill above Medraut's tame English village. Below us,
I could see the watch-fires flickering through the
morning mist and hear the lowing of their cows as
they waited to be milked. The place seemed peaceful
enough, but I remembered the spears and shields
and swords of the chief's huge hearth-companions
and their murderous shrieks as they'd tried to kill
me.

I turned to look at my own troops scuttling back
and forth through the oak trees under Flann's sharp,
warrior eyes. She wouldn't forebear to lay her stick
across a back if discipline broke down. There were so
few of them, I thought, to send against those fierce
Englishmen, even if the noise they'd made on the

road made them seem a great host. And the dust they threw up! A half century or more of soldiers, anyone seeing it would have thought.

I ruminated for a moment on the deceptiveness of appearances — goddesses who looked like cows or children, children and corpses who looked like birds. I touched the Lady-mark. A terrified girl who looked like the Lady of the Lake. Avalon's soldiers who looked like pigs.

And *were* pigs.

A dozen of the filthy creatures, skinny, half-starved beasts were snuffling the late summer mast — bark, beech nuts, acorns — and happily rooting up the sweet, wet grass. They'd found more to eat in a couple of days than they'd had in three years on Avalon. It would be hard, I knew, to get them away from here. Harder than it had been to board them into the carraghs. When they wouldn't go up the gangplank, Meredydd and I had to drive them in the opposite direction. Only then would the contrary brutes turn and run up it. And to get them off the boat, we had to tie a cord around their hind feet and yank backward — so they would pull forward down the plank. Hateful things. Worse than cows.

And, of course, to drive them across country was equally aggravating. The first thing they did when they left the boats was to scatter, lured by the smell of mast and fresh water. It was a good thing the Hound had brought us to the most isolated of Suth Seaxe coves because the squealing and cursing of the roundup was enough to have alarmed the entire English nation. Finally, though, we got them together and I set Macha to lead them away. They followed her easily enough once she dropped a bean or two in front of their hairy, red leader. The rest came following, grunting and greedy, as she continued to lay down that trail of beans halfway across Suth Seaxe.

At first we stayed on an old Roman road, cut straight and true through the chalky mainland dirt. Then the Hound led us into thick forest. For a while, I thought we were lost in that sunless deep, but soon she was finding her way along old Celtic paths known only to Avalon's Child Gatherers.

"Do you talk to wolves, now you're Chief Gatherer?" I asked as she pushed aside the nettles and berry bushes and thorn branches that clawed at us.

She laughed and didn't answer. But her laugh was like a howl in the night and I knew then she was truly Fand's heir. I would never again question her intelligence.

Now, two days later, standing in the forest above the English village, it was my own intelligence I questioned. How smart could one be to think she could send a herdlet of pigs against mailed and mighty English warriors? I shivered in fear.

Meanwhile, Flann and Macha patrolled the pigs and the Hound sniffed the air. "Elin's down there, all right," she said. And I thought of herb-scented hair and Italian musk. Of Elin's body against mine. Of the sweet, sharp cries of her pleasure. My courage returned.

"Where is she?" I asked. The Hound pointed to the little weaver's hut in which Nimue and I had been held.

"Can you smell out Medraut or does he stink the same as the English?" My nose crinkled as I thought of their rotten meat stench.

Once again, the Hound sniffed the wind. "Well, either he's not there or he's taken on their odor. He never was any too clean. The only smell I catch besides the English is Elin's."

I didn't let myself think Annis might be down there, too, smelling like the English.

"Where are their pigs? I can't see them." I recalled the pigsty being just outside the English chief's spiked fence.

"In the woods yonder." The Hound pointed to the far side of the village. "Flann and me'll go get 'em. The more the merrier."

I'd supposed that Flann and Macha were soul-friends, or about to be, from the giggling and groping that went on under the bearskin blanket in the Hall guardroom. But on the voyage, it became obvious that the Hound and Flann had discovered each other. And now they set off together, with a wave to me and the grinning Macha.

Soon they returned with half a dozen English pigs, much fatter and even meaner than our own. Just as we began the litany of Adventuring — "The Mother is; the Daughters go forth" — the English sow, a long-snouted white thing, attacked one of our young porklings. In his terror, he ran squealing into the brambles where he promptly choked on the hard old acorn he'd been slobbering over. When we finally tackled him, I had to take him by the heels and shake him till he coughed it up. Worse than cows!

We finished the litany finally and started down the hill toward the village, Flann now in the lead with the beans and wearing the English swineherd's foul-smelling clothes. (She and Hound had thumped him on the head and left him naked and tied to a tree.) As I'd hoped, no one paid us any mind when we went past the barns and byres and onto the village's single street.

The English were busy with their morning chores. Just outside the gate to the royal compound, near the horsetrough, a sleepy young milkmaid sat with her face pressed to the side of a brown cow. The slow rhythm of her milking matched that of the cow munching her cud. Further along the fence, leaning against it, a churl worked to attach a handle to his broken hoe. Carefully, he wound and re-wound a thong along its shaft.

In the street of daub and wattle houses, a woman sweeping her front step with a birch stick broom set up little whirlwinds of chalky dust. A tall tow-headed boy drove a gaggle of geese down the street behind an ox-cart heaped with fresh manure. And just in front of a baker carrying his loaves stacked up on a thick plank, a man I recognized as the chief himself walked with one of his hearth-companions. They were not armed, though they staggered a bit, perhaps the worse for a night of bragging in the meadhall.

Out in the fields, workers sang as they chopped back weeds. In the village, dogs barked and birds sang. Somewhere someone played a shepherd's pipe.

Medraut was not in evidence.

When we got to the middle of the village, Flann dipped into her bag of beans and flung out two handfuls like a Gardener sowing grain. Grunting, squealing, screaming, the pigs dashed after them.

The geese were the first to react. They hissed and hooted and flapped their wings as they spewed out of formation. Under the manure cart ran a gander, under the legs of the ox, who with a mighty leap of fear sent the cart crashing over, driver and manure dumped together in a stinking heap on the ground. The rest of the geese ran between the houses and out to the fields in a great cloud of feathers, dust, and noise, driving two children before them.

Meanwhile, the cow bawled twice, then broke away from the milkmaid, sending the girl head over butt into the dirt. The pail of milk, its creamy contents slopping down its wooden side, wobbled precariously for a moment then settled back unspilled. The cow, too, ran for safety in the fields, her tail up, heavy udders swaying.

The churl who'd been fixing the hoe joined the tow-headed gooseboy in hot pursuit of the white English sow as she headed for the royal compound. And the chief and his hearth-companion lumbered after a red pig who had somehow climbed into the horsetrough. The baker sat weeping next to his broken loaves.

There were pigs everywhere — striped ones, spotted ones, clean ones, dirty ones — big and little alike they streaked through the village. Flann and the Hound made the appearance of chasing them, even going after our young porkling as he ran past the woman with the broom and into her house. The woman screamed as the little thing shot by and then lay her broom hard across the pursuing Hound's shoulder. *"Swinhund!"* she yelled as she, too, flew into the house. Flann and the Hound came tearing back out again, in flight from the Englishwoman, who pelted them with dishes and chairs and even a straw bedtick. The pig apparently remained behind.

Macha, totally disabled with laughter, watched as the white sow, aided now by a Celtic confederate, tore down the royal gate, peered around the compound, then in a dignified manner advanced on the chief's herb garden.

By now the churls in the fields had thrown down their hoes and were hurrying toward the village. The piper had stopped, the birds no longer sang, and the dogs had entered the fray. The barking, squealing, bleating, squawking, and cursing in the village convinced me I wasn't noticed. So I left the English to protect their village from this plague of pigs and found my way to the weaver's hut.

The door stood slightly ajar. If there had been a guard, he was now engaged in chasing swine. Slowly, I pushed open the door and, drawing my sword, stepped inside.

Coming out of the sunlight, I was nearly blind. I blinked hard twice and my eyes began to adjust to the hut's dim interior. I recognized the weaver's footrest, but not the three shapes behind it. One, a long one, lay sprawled on the dirt floor. Another seemed to be kneeling before the third. When my eyes adjusted fully, I saw that the kneeling figure was Elin and whoever was in front of her had a hand around her throat.

"Go back, Argante!" Elin cried out and slapped off the hand.

Medraut — I saw him clearly now — kicked her away and advanced on me. His hand was drawn back and in it he held a Spanish sword.

I threw up my own sword and it clashed against his. For a moment, the swords locked. Then I stepped back and the footrest banged against my ankles. I fell and Medraut with me. He struck again. The blade sliced into my tunic sleeve, catching there long enough for me to bring my knee hard into his midsection.

The breath roared out of him and he flopped onto his back. I smashed my blade against his wrist and as his weapon dropped uselessly away, his face twisted in pain and his lips curled in a snarl of hatred. Desperate, he clawed at my face with his good hand, at my nose, at my lips, at anything he could rip or scratch or tear. He howled with the effort.

I ducked his hand and drew my sword back to slash it. But his hand was again in my face, nails raking my forehead, fingers jabbing my eye. I took my sword two-handed and sank it deep into his shoulder. He fell off me with a sob. I stood up, panting, and kicked him in the jaw. Outside, I could hear the pigs still squealing.

Then, Elin's arms were around me, her mouth on mine.

"You were a fool to come here," she said when we parted.

"Who's this?" I asked, prodding the other body with my toe. "And what happened to him?" He was obviously dead, but only recently; blood still bubbled from his throat like a slow, red spring.

"Some Englishman who was stupid enough to kill Caitlann and then too clumsy to get his prick out and hold me down at the same time. I got him with his own blade." She bent and pulled a knife out from under him. "Before Medraut got me," she added with a little smile.

Looking down at the dead man, I saw he was the giant who had helped capture Nimue and me those long years ago.

Behind us, Medraut began to groan a little. We turned back to him. He stared at me, eyes milkier than ever, and said, "Annis will have Avalon yet."

"Is she here?" I asked.

He sneered and said, "You've won, haven't you, sister? Well, you may have stopped *me* — for a time — but you cannot stop your drought."

Before I could respond, Elin was straddling him, the knife's point pressed to the hollow of his throat. She meant to kill him.

"Don't!" I cried.

For a moment, she knelt there, muscles tensed to ram the knife home. Then she laughed and stood up. "You and your awful family," she said, taking my hand. "Come on, then. I'd rather deal with the pigs."

Chapter Fifteen

We returned to the Island. With the rain. I felt its first driblet as we sailed into the Blue Bay. By the time we knelt in the Crystal Shrine to give thanks for our lives, it was falling over the Hall and the City, over all of Avalon. And it came not in a torrent to wash our hard red soil down to the sea; the rain embraced us like a mother, soft, warm, caressing.

That was in the spring. Before long, the new green was well sprouted and boatloads of grain and other stores arrived from Wales and Gaul. A good thing, too, because from the bawling and bleating and bellowing that filled the air, it seemed every cow and mare and ewe had come into season at once. The Healers cured the coughing sickness, women worked the fields and orchards of their steadings, the horses of the Lady Line again raced down the glens.

And I was hard at work trying to get it all organized. I kept the Nine in the Council Chamber half the night, hearing reports, laying plans, disposing of problems. Until Fedelm's loud snores and Eithne's noisy complaints would at last remind me there was such a thing as sleep. Elin helped me, of course, and glad I was for it. She was an experienced ruler who knew how to negotiate a way between the competing claims of Timber-women demanding the forests be replanted "Now!" and Millers insisting their dikes and sluices get repaired "Now!"

Sometimes Elin became so exhilarated by the task she would say, "It's a grand adventure, isn't it? This administration business." Leave it to Elin to find adventure wherever. But I noticed she'd left her own administrative "adventure" safely in the hands of greybearded bailiffs in Calchvynydd.

Elin and I were soul-friended that summer, along with Flann and the Hound. I would rather have had the ceremony be private, up in Tref Briga perhaps. But Elin wanted a big commotion in the Lady Hall at the Lughnasa festival. Deirdre agreed. "Briga and Meredydd and their bairns can as easily come down here," she said. "The rest of the Island, too. They'll need some ease by then."

I wondered just when it was that Deirdre became

so concerned with the well-being of bog-babies and Sheepherders and other such uncivilized creatures. But Arianrhod had recently visited from the north, to make sure Tref Arianrhod's sheep would be getting as much Welsh hay as Tref Ailma's cattle. She and Deirdre had disappeared for hours at a time, re-entering the Hall with a grin on Arianrhod's round face and Deirdre's grey hair in a terrible tangle. I had no idea Deirdre was interested in such things.

Anyway, Elin presented me with an elaborate scheme for getting not only all of Avalon to our soul-friending, but half the Celtic Realms as well. It would be a good opportunity, she said, to end Arthur's Irish war. Lughnasa was, after all, a time for bringing people together, for making alliances, political as well as personal.

Claudia, whose health Elin had restored, said the idea seemed logical. And, for the most part, the Nine also agreed. Except for the Hound. "I ain't swearing oath in a hall full of murdering mainlanders," she had declared. "Me and Flann'd as lief do it in the hog-house." Then they rode off to the Forest of Light where they said their words with only bear and badger to stand witness.

I understood their point. I certainly didn't want Arthur Pendragon next to me at the apple-cauldron when I told Elin: *If I break faith with you, may the sea swell over me, may the sky fall down upon me, may the ground rise up and take me.*

As for Arthur, he and his Great Sword could remain in Camelot! I would, however, welcome Lancelot or Perceval or whichever of his Companions he should choose to send as witness to our oath —

and to treat for peace with the High King of Ireland. And so, we would be soul-friended at Lughnasa.

One evening, a few days before the mainlanders arrived, Elin and I strolled out into the Lady Garden. Her hounds and terriers trailed after us as we examined the camellias' new leaves. "Eventually," she said, "I'll have to go back to Calchvynydd. For a spell, anyway. I believe my youngest sister would make the clan a good queen and —"

I put a finger on her lips. "That's a question for another time."

"There are other questions, too, Argante. And a sovereign must seek to solve them. Medraut, for instance."

Medraut. He'd no doubt headed straight for the Wastelands when I released him outside the English village. And I knew Annis would no doubt continue to use him against Avalon and the Celtic Realms as surely as she used the Grey Host.

I drew Elin to me. "Medraut and Annis are still problems, it's true. So is Calchvynydd. And so is feed for the Lady Line. And what to do about the apple crop. But, my love, as you would say yourself, that will be the adventure of it."

I looked up at the full moon rising over Avalon. "In the meantime," I said, breathing in the scent of Elin's hair. "In the meantime, the Mother is; the Daughters go forth."

A few of the publications of
THE NAIAD PRESS, INC.
P.O. Box 10543 • Tallahassee, Florida 32302
Phone (904) 539-5965
Mail orders welcome. Please include 15% postage.

IN THE GAME by Nikki Baker. 192 pp. A Virginia Kelly
mystery. First in a series.   ISBN 01-56280-004-3 $8.95

AVALON by Mary Jane Jones. 256 pp. A Lesbian Arthurian
romance.   ISBN 0-941483-96-7   9.95

STRANDED by Camarin Grae. 320 pp. Entertaining, riveting
adventure.   ISBN 0-941483-99-1   9.95

THE DAUGHTERS OF ARTEMIS by Lauren Wright Douglas.
240 pp. Third Caitlin Reece mystery.   ISBN 0-941483-95-9   8.95

CLEARWATER by Catherine Ennis. 176 pp. Romantic secrets
of a small Louisiana town.   ISBN 0-941483-65-7   8.95

THE HALLELUJAH MURDERS by Dorothy Tell. 176 pp.
Second Poppy Dillworth mystery.   ISBN 0-941483-88-6   8.95

ZETA BASE by Judith Alguire. 208 pp. Lesbian triangle
on a future Earth.   ISBN 0-941483-94-0   9.95

SECOND CHANCE by Jackie Calhoun. 256 pp. Contemporary
Lesbian lives and loves.   ISBN 0-941483-93-2   9.95

MURDER BY TRADITION by Katherine V. Forrest. 288 pp.
A Kate Delafield Mystery. 4th in a series.   ISBN 0-941483-89-4   18.95

BENEDICTION by Diane Salvatore. 272 pp. Striking,
contemporary romantic novel.   ISBN 0-941483-90-8   9.95

CALLING RAIN by Karen Marie Christa Minns. 240 pp.
Spellbinding, erotic love story   ISBN 0-941483-87-8   9.95

BLACK IRIS by Jeane Harris. 192 pp. Caroline's hidden past . . .
                                     ISBN 0-941483-68-1   8.95

TOUCHWOOD by Karin Kallmaker. 240 pp. Loving, May/
December romance.   ISBN 0-941483-76-2   8.95

BAYOU CITY SECRETS by Deborah Powell. 224 pp. A Hollis
Carpenter mystery. First in a series.   ISBN 0-941483-91-6   8.95

COP OUT by Claire McNab. 208 pp. 4th Det. Insp. Carol Ashton
mystery.   ISBN 0-941483-84-3   8.95

LODESTAR by Phyllis Horn. 224 pp. Romantic, fast-moving
adventure.   ISBN 0-941483-83-5   8.95

THE BEVERLY MALIBU by Katherine V. Forrest. 288 pp. A
Kate Delafield Mystery. 3rd in a series. (HC)   ISBN 0-941483-47-9   16.95
                               Paperback   ISBN 0-941483-48-7   9.95

THAT OLD STUDEBAKER by Lee Lynch. 272 pp. Andy's affair
with Regina and her attachment to her beloved car.
ISBN 0-941483-82-7   9.95

PASSION'S LEGACY by Lori Paige. 224 pp. Sarah is swept into
the arms of Augusta Pym in this delightful historical romance.
ISBN 0-941483-81-9   8.95

THE PROVIDENCE FILE by Amanda Kyle Williams. 256 pp.
Second espionage thriller featuring lesbian agent Madison McGuire
ISBN 0-941483-92-4   8.95

I LEFT MY HEART by Jaye Maiman. 320 pp. A Robin Miller
Mystery. First in a series.   ISBN 0-941483-72-X   9.95

THE PRICE OF SALT by Patricia Highsmith (writing as Claire
Morgan). 288 pp. Classic lesbian novel, first issued in 1952 . . .
acknowledged by its author under her own, very famous, name.
ISBN 1-56280-003-5   8.95

SIDE BY SIDE by Isabel Miller. 256 pp. From beloved author of
Patience and Sarah.   ISBN 0-941483-77-0   8.95

SOUTHBOUND by Sheila Ortiz Taylor. 240 pp. Hilarious sequel
to *Faultline.*   ISBN 0-941483-78-9   8.95

STAYING POWER: LONG TERM LESBIAN COUPLES
by Susan E. Johnson. 352 pp. Joys of coupledom.
ISBN 0-941-483-75-4   12.95

SLICK by Camarin Grae. 304 pp. Exotic, erotic adventure.
ISBN 0-941483-74-6   9.95

NINTH LIFE by Lauren Wright Douglas. 256 pp. A Caitlin
Reece mystery. 2nd in a series.   ISBN 0-941483-50-9   8.95

PLAYERS by Robbi Sommers. 192 pp. Sizzling, erotic novel.
ISBN 0-941483-73-8   8.95

MURDER AT RED ROOK RANCH by Dorothy Tell. 224 pp.
First Poppy Dillworth adventure.   ISBN 0-941483-80-0   8.95

LESBIAN SURVIVAL MANUAL by Rhonda Dicksion.
112 pp. Cartoons!   ISBN 0-941483-71-1   8.95

A ROOM FULL OF WOMEN by Elisabeth Nonas. 256 pp.
Contemporary Lesbian lives.   ISBN 0-941483-69-X   8.95

MURDER IS RELATIVE by Karen Saum. 256 pp. The first
Brigid Donovan mystery.   ISBN 0-941483-70-3   8.95

PRIORITIES by Lynda Lyons 288 pp. Science fiction with
a twist.   ISBN 0-941483-66-5   8.95

THEME FOR DIVERSE INSTRUMENTS by Jane Rule. 208
pp. Powerful romantic lesbian stories.   ISBN 0-941483-63-0   8.95

LESBIAN QUERIES by Hertz & Ertman. 112 pp. The questions
you were too embarrassed to ask.   ISBN 0-941483-67-3   8.95

CLUB 12 by Amanda Kyle Williams. 288 pp. Espionage thriller
featuring a lesbian agent! ISBN 0-941483-64-9 8.95

DEATH DOWN UNDER by Claire McNab. 240 pp. 3rd Det.
Insp. Carol Ashton mystery. ISBN 0-941483-39-8 8.95

MONTANA FEATHERS by Penny Hayes. 256 pp. Vivian and
Elizabeth find love in frontier Montana. ISBN 0-941483-61-4 8.95

CHESAPEAKE PROJECT by Phyllis Horn. 304 pp. Jessie &
Meredith in perilous adventure. ISBN 0-941483-58-4 8.95

LIFESTYLES by Jackie Calhoun. 224 pp. Contemporary Lesbian
lives and loves. ISBN 0-941483-57-6 8.95

VIRAGO by Karen Marie Christa Minns. 208 pp. Darsen has
chosen Ginny. ISBN 0-941483-56-8 8.95

WILDERNESS TREK by Dorothy Tell. 192 pp. Six women on
vacation learning "new" skills. ISBN 0-941483-60-6 8.95

MURDER BY THE BOOK by Pat Welch. 256 pp. A Helen
Black Mystery. First in a series. ISBN 0-941483-59-2 8.95

BERRIGAN by Vicki P. McConnell. 176 pp. Youthful Lesbian —
romantic, idealistic Berrigan. ISBN 0-941483-55-X 8.95

LESBIANS IN GERMANY by Lillian Faderman & B. Eriksson.
128 pp. Fiction, poetry, essays. ISBN 0-941483-62-2 8.95

THERE'S SOMETHING I'VE BEEN MEANING TO TELL
YOU Ed. by Loralee MacPike. 288 pp. Gay men and lesbians
coming out to their children. ISBN 0-941483-44-4 9.95
ISBN 0-941483-54-1 16.95

LIFTING BELLY by Gertrude Stein. Ed. by Rebecca Mark. 104
pp. Erotic poetry. ISBN 0-941483-51-7 8.95
ISBN 0-941483-53-3 14.95

ROSE PENSKI by Roz Perry. 192 pp. Adult lovers in a long-term
relationship. ISBN 0-941483-37-1 8.95

AFTER THE FIRE by Jane Rule. 256 pp. Warm, human novel
by this incomparable author. ISBN 0-941483-45-2 8.95

SUE SLATE, PRIVATE EYE by Lee Lynch. 176 pp. The gay
folk of Peacock Alley are *all cats*. ISBN 0-941483-52-5 8.95

CHRIS by Randy Salem. 224 pp. Golden oldie. Handsome Chris
and her adventures. ISBN 0-941483-42-8 8.95

THREE WOMEN by March Hastings. 232 pp. Golden oldie. A
triangle among wealthy sophisticates. ISBN 0-941483-43-6 8.95

RICE AND BEANS by Valeria Taylor. 232 pp. Love and
romance on poverty row. ISBN 0-941483-41-X 8.95

PLEASURES by Robbi Sommers. 204 pp. Unprecedented
eroticism. ISBN 0-941483-49-5 8.95

EDGEWISE by Camarin Grae. 372 pp. Spellbinding
adventure.   ISBN 0-941483-19-3   9.95

FATAL REUNION by Claire McNab. 224 pp. 2nd Det. Inspec.
Carol Ashton mystery.   ISBN 0-941483-40-1   8.95

KEEP TO ME STRANGER by Sarah Aldridge. 372 pp. Romance
set in a department store dynasty.   ISBN 0-941483-38-X   9.95

HEARTSCAPE by Sue Gambill. 204 pp. American lesbian in
Portugal.   ISBN 0-941483-33-9   8.95

IN THE BLOOD by Lauren Wright Douglas. 252 pp. Lesbian
science fiction adventure fantasy   ISBN 0-941483-22-3   8.95

THE BEE'S KISS by Shirley Verel. 216 pp. Delicate, delicious
romance.   ISBN 0-941483-36-3   8.95

RAGING MOTHER MOUNTAIN by Pat Emmerson. 264 pp.
Furosa Firechild's adventures in Wonderland. ISBN 0-941483-35-5   8.95

IN EVERY PORT by Karin Kallmaker. 228 pp. Jessica's sexy,
adventuresome travels.   ISBN 0-941483-37-7   8.95

OF LOVE AND GLORY by Evelyn Kennedy. 192 pp. Exciting
WWII romance.   ISBN 0-941483-32-0   8.95

CLICKING STONES by Nancy Tyler Glenn. 288 pp. Love
transcending time.   ISBN 0-941483-31-2   9.95

SURVIVING SISTERS by Gail Pass. 252 pp. Powerful love
story.   ISBN 0-941483-16-9   8.95

SOUTH OF THE LINE by Catherine Ennis. 216 pp. Civil War
adventure.   ISBN 0-941483-29-0   8.95

WOMAN PLUS WOMAN by Dolores Klaich. 300 pp. Supurb
Lesbian overview.   ISBN 0-941483-28-2   9.95

SLOW DANCING AT MISS POLLY'S by Sheila Ortiz Taylor.
96 pp. Lesbian Poetry   ISBN 0-941483-30-4   7.95

DOUBLE DAUGHTER by Vicki P. McConnell. 216 pp. A Nyla
Wade Mystery, third in the series.   ISBN 0-941483-26-6   8.95

HEAVY GILT by Delores Klaich. 192 pp. Lesbian detective/
disappearing homophobes/upper class gay society.

                                             ISBN 0-941483-25-8   8.95

THE FINER GRAIN by Denise Ohio. 216 pp. Brilliant young
college lesbian novel.   ISBN 0-941483-11-8   8.95

THE AMAZON TRAIL by Lee Lynch. 216 pp. Life, travel & lore
of famous lesbian author.   ISBN 0-941483-27-4   8.95

HIGH CONTRAST by Jessie Lattimore. 264 pp. Women of the
Crystal Palace.   ISBN 0-941483-17-7   8.95

OCTOBER OBSESSION by Meredith More. Josie's rich, secret
Lesbian life.   ISBN 0-941483-18-5   8.95

THE PEARLS by Shelley Smith. 176 pp. Passion and fun in
the Caribbean sun.   ISBN 0-930044-93-2   7.95

MAGDALENA by Sarah Aldridge. 352 pp. Epic Lesbian novel
set on three continents.   ISBN 0-930044-99-1   8.95

THE BLACK AND WHITE OF IT by Ann Allen Shockley.
144 pp. Short stories.   ISBN 0-930044-96-7   7.95

SAY JESUS AND COME TO ME by Ann Allen Shockley. 288
pp. Contemporary romance.   ISBN 0-930044-98-3   8.95

LOVING HER by Ann Allen Shockley. 192 pp. Romantic love
story.   ISBN 0-930044-97-5   7.95

MURDER AT THE NIGHTWOOD BAR by Katherine V.
Forrest. 240 pp. A Kate Delafield mystery. Second in a series.
                                      ISBN 0-930044-92-4   9.95

ZOE'S BOOK by Gail Pass. 224 pp. Passionate, obsessive love
story.   ISBN 0-930044-95-9   7.95

WINGED DANCER by Camarin Grae. 228 pp. Erotic Lesbian
adventure story.   ISBN 0-930044-88-6   8.95

PAZ by Camarin Grae. 336 pp. Romantic Lesbian adventurer
with the power to change the world.   ISBN 0-930044-89-4   8.95

SOUL SNATCHER by Camarin Grae. 224 pp. A puzzle, an
adventure, a mystery — Lesbian romance.   ISBN 0-930044-90-8   8.95

THE LOVE OF GOOD WOMEN by Isabel Miller. 224 pp.
Long-awaited new novel by the author of the beloved *Patience
and Sarah*.   ISBN 0-930044-81-9   8.95

THE HOUSE AT PELHAM FALLS by Brenda Weathers. 240
pp. Suspenseful Lesbian ghost story. ISBN 0-930044-79-7   7.95

HOME IN YOUR HANDS by Lee Lynch. 240 pp. More stories
from the author of *Old Dyke Tales*. ISBN 0-930044-80-0   7.95

EACH HAND A MAP by Anita Skeen. 112 pp. Real-life poems
that touch us all.   ISBN 0-930044-82-7   6.95

SURPLUS by Sylvia Stevenson. 342 pp. A classic early Lesbian
novel.   ISBN 0-930044-78-9   7.95

PEMBROKE PARK by Michelle Martin. 256 pp. Derring-do
and daring romance in Regency England.   ISBN 0-930044-77-0   7.95

THE LONG TRAIL by Penny Hayes. 248 pp. Vivid adventures
of two women in love in the old west. ISBN 0-930044-76-2   8.95

HORIZON OF THE HEART by Shelley Smith. 192 pp. Hot
romance in summertime New England.   ISBN 0-930044-75-4   7.95

AN EMERGENCE OF GREEN by Katherine V. Forrest. 288
pp. Powerful novel of sexual discovery.   ISBN 0-930044-69-X   9.95

THE LESBIAN PERIODICALS INDEX edited by Claire
Potter. 432 pp. Author & subject index.   ISBN 0-930044-74-6   29.95

TOOTHPICK HOUSE by Lee Lynch. 264 pp. Love between
two Lesbians of different classes.   ISBN 0-930044-45-2   7.95

MADAME AURORA by Sarah Aldridge. 256 pp. Historical
novel featuring a charismatic "seer."   ISBN 0-930044-44-4   7.95

CURIOUS WINE by Katherine V. Forrest. 176 pp. Passionate
Lesbian love story, a best-seller.   ISBN 0-930044-43-6   8.95

BLACK LESBIAN IN WHITE AMERICA by Anita Cornwell.
141 pp. Stories, essays, autobiography.   ISBN 0-930044-41-X   7.95

CONTRACT WITH THE WORLD by Jane Rule. 340 pp.
Powerful, panoramic novel of gay life.   ISBN 0-930044-28-2   9.95

MRS. PORTER'S LETTER by Vicki P. McConnell. 224 pp.
The first Nyla Wade mystery.   ISBN 0-930044-29-0   7.95

TO THE CLEVELAND STATION by Carol Anne Douglas.
192 pp. Interracial Lesbian love story.   ISBN 0-930044-27-4   6.95

THE NESTING PLACE by Sarah Aldridge. 224 pp. A
three-woman triangle — love conquers all!   ISBN 0-930044-26-6   7.95

THIS IS NOT FOR YOU by Jane Rule. 284 pp. A letter to a
beloved is also an intricate novel.   ISBN 0-930044-25-8   8.95

FAULTLINE by Sheila Ortiz Taylor. 140 pp. Warm, funny,
literate story of a startling family.   ISBN 0-930044-24-X   6.95

ANNA'S COUNTRY by Elizabeth Lang. 208 pp. A woman
finds her Lesbian identity.   ISBN 0-930044-19-3   8.95

PRISM by Valerie Taylor. 158 pp. A love affair between two
women in their sixties.   ISBN 0-930044-18-5   6.95

THE MARQUISE AND THE NOVICE by Victoria Ramstetter.
108 pp. A Lesbian Gothic novel.   ISBN 0-930044-16-9   6.95

OUTLANDER by Jane Rule. 207 pp. Short stories and essays
by one of our finest writers.   ISBN 0-930044-17-7   8.95

ALL TRUE LOVERS by Sarah Aldridge. 292 pp. Romantic
novel set in the 1930s and 1940s.   ISBN 0-930044-10-X   8.95

A WOMAN APPEARED TO ME by Renee Vivien. 65 pp. A
classic; translated by Jeannette H. Foster.   ISBN 0-930044-06-1   5.00

CYTHEREA'S BREATH by Sarah Aldridge. 240 pp. Romantic
novel about women's entrance into medicine.
                                              ISBN 0-930044-02-9   6.95

TOTTIE by Sarah Aldridge. 181 pp. Lesbian romance in the
turmoil of the sixties.   ISBN 0-930044-01-0   6.95

THE LATECOMER by Sarah Aldridge. 107 pp. A delicate love
story.   ISBN 0-930044-00-2   6.95

ODD GIRL OUT by Ann Bannon.   ISBN 0-930044-83-5   5.95
I AM A WOMAN 84-3; WOMEN IN THE SHADOWS 85-1;   each
JOURNEY TO A WOMAN 86-X; BEEBO BRINKER 87-8. Golden
oldies about life in Greenwich Village.

JOURNEY TO FULFILLMENT, A WORLD WITHOUT MEN, and   3.95
RETURN TO LESBOS. All by Valerie Taylor   each

These are just a few of the many Naiad Press titles — we are the oldest and
largest lesbian/feminist publishing company in the world. Please request a
complete catalog. We offer personal service; we encourage and welcome direct
mail orders from individuals who have limited access to bookstores carrying
our publications.